# HAUNTING SHADOWS

Within days of Emma's arrival in Cornwall after her whirlwind marriage to Alex Crawley, they repeatedly see a woman resembling Louise, his drowned first wife. As Rachel, the unwelcoming nanny/housekeeper, refuses to let her cope with Alex's young son, Emma takes a job as receptionist to Brian Pendower at the harbourside inn, despite Alex's disapproval. Tormented by guilt, Alex tells Emma he was responsible for Louise's death — but is she really dead? Was Brian her lover? In a terrifying ordeal, Emma finally discovers the secret of Louise.

REBECCA BENNETT

# HAUNTING SHADOWS

*Complete and Unabridged*

# LINFORD
*Leicester*

First published in Great Britain in 1991

First Linford Edition
published 2016

A catalogue record for this book is available
from the British Library.

ISBN 978–1–4448–2837–5

Published by
F. A. Thorpe (Publishing)
Anstey, Leicestershire

Set by Words & Graphics Ltd.
Anstey, Leicestershire
Printed and bound in Great Britain by
T. J. International Ltd., Padstow, Cornwall

This book is printed on acid-free paper

# 1

Emma first met Alexander Crawley on a Monday morning early in May. By Tuesday evening she knew she was in love with him. For a girl who had always been so level-headed and sensible all her life, it was an unbelievable thing to happen, but love can be like that sometimes.

For nearly six years, Emma had worked in the offices of Cavendish & Company, ever since she left secretarial college with a handful of certificates and letter of reference declaring her to be efficient, reliable and hard-working.

During that time this had proved to be a correct assessment and she had risen up through the firm until now she was personal assistant to Henry Cavendish himself — a job no one envied.

When Alexander Crawley arrived on

that Monday morning, Emma looked up with her usual welcoming smile and felt it waver under the piercing blue stare that met hers.

The dark-haired, chisel-faced man in his early thirties, wearing an immaculate grey pin-striped suit, towering over her, didn't smile back.

'Mr Crawley?' Her voice was unusually breathless.

He nodded impatiently, glancing at his watch.

'Would you like some coffee while you wait?'

'My appointment's for nine o'clock,' he pointed out tersely.

'And you're a little early, Mr Crawley,' she replied smoothly. 'Mr Cavendish hasn't arrived yet, but he shouldn't be long. The traffic's pretty bad at this time of the day.'

The taut planes of Alex Crawley's face relaxed slightly as he said, 'I will have that coffee then,' and Emma was acutely aware of his appraising eyes watching her as she poured it from the stand near her desk and turned to hand him the cup.

'Will you have dinner with me tonight?'

The question was so unexpected that the coffee almost slopped over when she passed it to him.

'I beg your pardon?'

'You do eat, don't you?' he enquired, his gaze skimming swiftly over the warm cluster of her red-gold hair, lingering for a brief second on the swell of her tiny breasts, before continuing down past the curving smoothness of her hips to the trim, slim ankles. 'Being so slender makes me wonder.'

'Yes, but . . . ' Emma hesitated, suddenly overwhelmed by a tumult of feelings she couldn't quite define.

'I'm on my own up here in London, you see.' His blue eyes crinkled as he smiled at her. 'And I could do with some company.'

Well, she thought, at least he's honest, but before she could give her reply the door opened and Henry

Cavendish came in, instantly filling the room with his presence.

'So you've arrived already, Alex. I should've known. You never were one to waste time, were you?' he boomed, taking the other man's hand in a firm handshake and leading him into his office.

'I'll have a cup of that coffee too, Emma, then I'd like you to come in and take notes on our discussion.'

Still stunned by the impact of Alexander Crawley and his invitation, Emma automatically did as she was told, picking up her notepad and carrying it, with the cup, into the adjoining room where the two men were deep in conversation, the wide desk already scattered with typewritten pages and diagrams.

'Alex owns a civil engineering firm in Truro, Emma, so I'm hoping we can contract out some of the work on that new bypass we're going to build down there. He'll be here in London for a few days, and I'd like you to give him any help you can.'

The strong blue gaze was turned in Emma's direction and a slight smile eased the sharp contours of his face as Alex looked at her.

'Of course, Mr Cavendish,' she replied, flipping over the pages of her notebook, trying to ignore the rush of colour that flared into her cheeks.

It was a long day. Emma's wrist ached from the fast pace as her pen took endless pages of notes while the two men argued. Henry Cavendish was a hard man to convince but she could see that even he was impressed by the precise factual detail and knowledge with which Alex countered his every question.

Sandwiches were sent in at midday from the pub across the road and the battle raged on all afternoon. By half-past four Emma knew she was going to be working late that evening to get everything typed up ready for the following day's meeting.

She was still frantically typing at a

quarter-past seven when her office door opened and Alex's handsome angular face appeared.

'Good heavens, young lady. Is this really necessary? I thought we were eating together. Do you realise what the time is?'

Emma was surprised to see him.

'You haven't been waiting for me, have you?'

'Of course I have. I invited you to dinner, didn't I? Although to be honest I have been putting the time to good use reading up a few of these reports Henry gave me. It'll be useful ammunition for tomorrow when I have to meet some of the others.'

'Maybe you should go and eat,' Emma suggested. 'I'll be quite a while yet. There are at least a couple more pages to type and then I'll have to photocopy everything.'

'Where's the machine?' His dark eyebrows were raised in question.

'In the next office,' she replied.

'Are these the pages to be done?' he

asked, picking up a sheaf of papers.

She nodded.

'How many copies?'

'Six. One each for you and Mr Cavendish, three for the site managers at tomorrow's meeting and one for the file.'

'Right then,' he said briskly. 'Bring me the rest of the pages when you've typed them.'

'But Mr Crawley . . . ' she began, only to find her voice drowned by the whirr of the photocopier from the next room as it began to print out.

He was leaning on the machine, jacket slung casually over the back of a chair, the sleeves of his crisp white shirt rolled up, the knot of his navy silk tie loosened, gathering the sheets and stacking them neatly into six piles on the table, when Emma took in the final pages.

'It's nearly eight o'clock and I'm starving,' he said, sliding them on to the machine and keying it into life again. 'You staple those together while I phone and reserve a table. It won't take long to reach my hotel if we can get a taxi.'

'Are you quite sure — ' she started to say, but once again he cut her off abruptly.

'Look, young lady. All I'm asking is for you to have dinner with me. Do I have to go down on bended knees or something? If you have another date, then please say so.'

'No,' she replied. 'I haven't, it's just that . . . '

He gave a sigh of exasperation.

'Just get on with that photocopying, will you, while I go and make the phone call.'

★ ★ ★

'Have you ever been to Cornwall?'

They'd reached the cheese and biscuits stage of their meal and, warm with wine, Emma was at last beginning to relax a little in his company.

She shook her head.

'I suppose you're the sort of girl who spends her holidays on sun-drenched beaches abroad?'

'Usually. I do like to get a tan.'

'You can get one just as easily in my part of the country and I can assure you it's far more beautiful than any beach you'll find elsewhere in the world — although maybe I'm biased. I love it there so much.'

'Well, you certainly have a fantastic tan to prove it,' Emma smiled, staring at the deeply bronzed skin that made his eyes appear even more blue in the soft candlelit glow of the room.

'Let's take the rest of the wine up to my room and continue our conversation there,' he said, suddenly rising to his feet and reaching out his hand to take hers.

Slivers of alarm shot warningly through Emma. So that was his idea, was it?

'I think it's time I left,' she announced firmly.

'But it's early yet,' he protested.

'Look, there's almost half a bottle left. It's far too good to waste. I'll order coffee to be sent up.'

'Thank you, Mr Crawley, but no,' she replied, picking up her bag.

His tanned face crinkled into a broad smile.

'Surely you don't imagine I'm about to seduce you, do you? Really, Emma! That kind of thing only happens in romantic novels. Men don't go around leaping into bed at the slightest provocation — not when they've had a day like I've just had, I can assure you.'

He grinned at her wickedly.

'Although I must admit the idea does appeal to me.'

'I really must be going,' she said, unable to resist smiling back at him. 'It's quite a way on the train.'

A look of concern creased his face.

'I'm sorry, I never thought. Where exactly do you live? I'll get a taxi for you.'

'No,' she protested. 'It's quite all right.'

'Then let me walk you to the station. I could do with a breath of air after being cooped up all day in that office. I must say that's something I miss in London — clear sea air.'

Clasping her hand in his, he hurried her along the streets so fast that she almost had to run to keep up with his long-legged stride.

At the station he looked down at her and said lightly, 'I've enjoyed this evening. Can we do the same tomorrow?'

And seeing the heart-stopping expression in his eyes, Emma could only answer with a breathless yes.

★ ★ ★

The next day she was up early, washing her hair, ironing her prettiest dress, putting on her make-up with extra care.

Why am I bothering? she asked herself, slipping her feet into a pair of high-heeled shoes that made her legs look twice as long, but the quickening of her pulse as she sped along the sun-bright morning streets told her the reason.

Alex was already in the office when she arrived and glanced up from behind a pair of thick-rimmed spectacles to smile at her over the top of a pile of files and papers.

'Hullo, Emma.'

The husky tone of his voice made her body melt.

She wasn't included in the meeting that day and tried desperately to concentrate on her work, but her mind kept remembering the deep blue of Alex's gaze and the welcoming expression in his eyes when he saw her again until she found herself making more mistakes than she'd ever done before.

This is ridiculous, she told herself sternly. I've only just met the man. I know nothing about him. He's a total stranger.

But she knew that didn't matter one bit. Her whole life was never going to be the same again.

While they ate together that evening, their heads grew closer until they were almost touching across the table and when Alex reached out to pour more wine into her glass, their hands met, making Emma jerk away suddenly as though his fingers were on fire. For a moment they seemed to burn into her skin, sending a tingle of shock throughout the whole of her body and he gave her a startled look, reading the message she couldn't disguise in her eyes.

When this time he suggested coffee in his room, she rose eagerly to her feet, but once there, in the intimacy of such enclosed seclusion, she felt confused and nervous. There was only one chair and a wide double bed, its duvet and pillows smooth and soft, increasing her anxiety.

Alex seemed to sense her dismay and guided her into the chair, then with a slight smile produced a stool from the adjoining bathroom on which he perched his long lean frame, moving the tray of coffee onto a small bedside table between them.

'I go back to Cornwall tomorrow, Emma,' he said and she tried to veil her disappointment as she stared back at him, tears stinging behind her eyes.

'Oh,' was all she could manage to say in a pathetic whisper. So everything's over before it's even begun, she thought.

'But I'll be returning in a couple of weeks to finalise all the details with Henry and sign the contract. When I do . . . will you marry me?'

'Marry you?'

Her brain was churning, not believing, not understanding. She must be drunk, deluded, going insane.

'I don't want to lose you, Emma.'

'But we've only just met,' she blurted out. 'We don't even know each other. How can you ask such a thing?'

'Because I've fallen in love with you,' he said simply, reaching out to draw her into his arms, his mouth moving slowly, caressing its way across her skin.

She felt his lips meet then brush hers, lightly at first, growing more intense, beginning to burn as her mouth parted, the warmth of her body moulding itself against his.

'And I think, maybe, you feel the same way too,' he whispered, tangling his fingers in her hair while he pulled her even closer with a fierceness that made her pulse with excitement.

'But how . . . why . . . ' she murmured when he finally released her.

'It happens,' he smiled, smoothing her hair with gentle fingers. 'Two lost souls, waiting. And then, at last, they meet. I knew, as soon as I saw you . . . '

And so did I, she thought, letting her lips answer for her.

★   ★   ★

'Two weeks,' he said as she leaned in through the carriage window, never wanting to let go of his hand. 'Then I'll be back.'

Two weeks. The time yawned into the

distance like an empty cave.

Two whole weeks.

And at the end of it, they would be married. It didn't seem possible. What was she doing? Marriage was for ever.

For ever. The thought filled her with delight.

There was so much to be done. Her flat was only rented, but even so her own belongings had to be packed. And a dress for the wedding had to be chosen. A trousseau. Did girls have such a thing any more?

Her parents were horrified at the sudden rush.

'You're not . . . ' her mother asked, her face anxious, when Emma went there for the weekend.

'No, I'm not pregnant,' she laughed, giving her a hug.

'But darling, it's all so sudden. How long have you known him?'

'Two days.'

'Two days! Oh, Emma darling, are you sure you know what you're doing?'

'Positive,' she replied.

16

'But two days . . . really, darling. How can you know?'

'I know.'

'Don't you think you should wait a little longer? After all, marriage is a big step, Emma.'

'Do stop worrying, Mum, and help me get everything ready.'

'Cornwall's so far away too,' her mother wailed. 'We're never going to see anything of you.'

'It's not the other side of the world,' Emma declared laughingly, 'and think of all the marvellous holidays you'll be able to have down there with us.'

'I really do think you should give yourself a little more time to decide, darling. What do you know about this Alexander?'

What did she know? Only that he was the most wonderful, delightful, attractive man she'd ever met — and that there was no one else she would love as much again. Surely that was enough?

Her mother didn't seem to agree

though and at the end of the weekend they parted on rather distant terms, which filled Emma with regret.

But then how could her mother remember what falling in love was like any more? She'd been married for nearly twenty-five years.

Henry Cavendish showed his displeasure in more positive terms.

'Don't be so bloody ridiculous, Emma,' he bellowed. 'Handing in your notice — I've never heard such nonsense. When I asked young Crawley to come up to London, I didn't think he was going to entice away my secretary.'

'I'm sorry, Mr Cavendish.'

Emma felt quite wretched. She enjoyed her job and would be sad to leave it, but she had no other choice.

'He's a likeable enough young fellow, I'll grant you that, and extremely capable, but as for marrying him, really Emma, you hardly know the man.'

Why couldn't any of them understand? she raged inwardly.

'I love him, Mr Cavendish,' she stated firmly.

'Love!' he roared. 'You don't know the meaning of the word, young lady. You're still a mere child!'

Emma bristled with indignation.

'I'm nearly twenty-three,' she protested.

'As I said, a mere child,' he replied with a slight twinkle in his eye. 'Look, Emma, my dear. I think too highly of you to want to see you hurt. Don't you feel you're rushing into things rather? Alex is a very impulsive young man. Always has been — and I've known him since he was a boy — always out to get what he wants, come what may. But marriage is a serious business, you know.'

'I realise that and I've thought about it extremely carefully,' she told him decisively. 'I've no doubts at all, Mr Cavendish.'

Near the end of her final week, he looked at her sadly and shook his head.

'Well, my dear. I shall be sorry to lose you, but I wish you every happiness.

And, of course, Jamie does need a mother.'

'Jamie?'

Emma stared back at him in bewilderment.

'Alex's son. Didn't he tell you about him?'

She shook her head bleakly.

Alex had been married before. I should've realised, she thought, angry at her own naïveté. A man like Alex couldn't have remained single for so long. But a child . . .

'James is a delightful little chap. Extremely bright too. He must be about five or six by now. I'm sure you'll get along splendidly,' Henry was saying, but Emma hardly heard him.

'When was Alex divorced?' she questioned.

'Divorced? Oh, Alex isn't divorced, my dear. Louise is dead. She was drowned about three years ago. It quite devastated him. He was devoted to her. A lovely girl.'

The words echoed hollowly round

her, each one filling her with bleakness.

Why hadn't Alex ever told her, or even said he'd been married before?

But then, they'd spent so little time together. Two days. Not even that. Just a few brief hours alone — when the past hadn't been thought of, only the future.

'I'm surprised Alex hasn't mentioned her death though. It caused him a great deal of unhappiness at the time.'

Emma felt drained of all emotion, a numb chill spreading through her.

*Devoted to his wife*, Henry had said. The words beat into her. Was she only to take second place in Alex's heart? *Jamie needs a mother*. Was that the reason for the haste? And yet, remembering those hours together, the intensity of his kisses, she felt sure Alex loved her. Or was it merely the fact that she was there, alone with him — and obviously so willing? But he didn't have to ask her to marry him, did he? Not unless he truly loved and wanted her.

Emma slept very little that night, thoughts pounding in her head, doubts filling her.

She was desperate to talk to Alex, to find out the answers, but she didn't know his telephone number or even his address. It wasn't something she'd thought about in those few pulsing hours together. Henry could easily have told her, but how could she admit such a thing to him? It would only convince him further of the futility of their marriage.

When Alex phoned, the night before he was due to return to London, the sound of his voice filled her with such intense happiness that all her worries vanished instantly. This was the man she was going to marry. Nothing else mattered.

'I love you, Emma,' he told her.

'I love you too,' she replied.

'I've got the special licence. Everything's arranged. I can't wait to be with you again.'

'Alex.'

'Yes,' he answered.

She paused, searching to find the right words.

'It doesn't matter,' she said at last. Nothing mattered — only Alex.

'Till tomorrow then.'

'Tomorrow,' she breathed.

The phone still trembled in her fingers and she stared down without seeing it.

Why couldn't I ask him? she wondered. Was it because I was afraid of the answer? That he loved Louise so much.

⋆ ⋆ ⋆

The next day, when he came into her office, it was as if her heart would burst with love for him. No man had ever made her feel like this before.

And when he bent to kiss her, she wanted to clasp her arms round his neck and hold him close, but with Henry waiting in the office next door, she didn't dare to do so.

The rest of the afternoon was a blur, clearing her desk, tidying everything, smiling mechanically at those who came to say goodbye and wish her good luck. Alex was so near and yet she couldn't see him, only hear the deep tones of his voice in the adjoining room.

This time tomorrow, she thought, I'll be his wife.

*His second wife*, came a nagging little echo inside of her.

But Louise was dead. It didn't matter. It wasn't like a divorce where she'd still be there, somewhere, flesh and blood that could appear at any time.

Louise was dead.

'I'd always dreamed of you having a white wedding,' her mother murmured when they arrived at the square brick register office building next morning. 'In that pretty little church in the village.'

And so had I, Emma thought, remembering.

She, too, had dreamed of the coolness of silk falling in soft folds round her. A haze of veiling misting her vision. A procession of tiny bridesmaids. Flowers cascading from every corner of the church. Bells pealing out over the melodic notes of the organ. Stained glass windows. Sunbeams dancing. Everyone from the village there, listening in hushed silence as she made her vows.

The registrar muttered the solemn words in a toneless voice as if he'd said them so many times before, they held no meaning for him any more.

She heard Alex repeat them, felt the cool gold of the ring slip onto her finger, the pressure of his hand as it held hers, and the brush of his lips as he kissed her.

Her parents watched, stiff-faced, her mother's eyes tear-filled.

Henry was his usual bluff self, loud with congratulations, slapping Alex on the back with a heavy hand.

'You're a lucky chap, Alex, but I can

assure you that if I'd been forty years younger, you wouldn't have stood a chance. Quite a lad, I was then. Now, lead me to the booze.'

They had a quiet lunch in a nearby hotel, just a dozen or so there, mainly friends she'd worked with for so long. There hadn't been time to organise more and Alex's parents were too old to make the long journey from Cornwall.

'You'll meet them soon, darling,' he assured her when at last they kissed their guests farewell and climbed the hotel stairs to the room he'd booked for the night.

Emma stared round it with wide eyes, taking in the plain wooden furniture, the pale pattern of roses on the wallpaper, the pink carpet darkly edged against the walls, the thick velvet curtains that didn't quite meet across the window; the low bed piled with white pillows and a deep red eider-down.

How shall I tell him? she wondered. Will he think me naïve?

She turned to Alex, watching him hang his slate-grey jacket on a hanger and begin to loosen his tie.

'I've never . . . ' she began, but his lips silenced her words.

'Don't worry,' he whispered, his fingers feathering her skin as he unzipped the soft wool of her dress. 'I love you, Emma, and I always will.'

# 2

When eventually Alex slept, Emma lay beside him, still breathless from their love-making, her body warm and relaxed from his gentle touch. She was bewildered by the force of her own emotions, hardly able to believe that she was capable of such intense feeling.

She could hear the soft sound of Alex's breathing and remembered how different it had been only minutes earlier; feel his body rest lightly against hers, knowing its passion and strength; see the outline of his head dark on the fullness of the pillow.

With one tentative hand, she reached out to smooth the ruffled hair away from his broad forehead and smiled as he snuggled his face deeper into the covers. My husband, she thought contentedly, letting her fingers travel softly down the hard bone to his jaw.

She saw his lips move and leaned nearer to hear the word he murmured.

'Louise.'

Horrified, her body stiffened and she drew away from him, tears burning her eyes. Was that who he was thinking of when he held her in his arms? Was that who he was really making love to so passionately? And for the rest of the long silent night, Emma's tears scalded the pillow.

The gentle persuasion of his touch woke her, turning her to him, his lips brushing her skin tantalisingly, rousing her into desire as she lay there sleepily gazing up at him, forgetting.

And then it all came back to her, making her tense away from him.

'Why didn't you tell me you'd been married before, Alex?' she asked.

His hand stilled on her breast, his blue eyes narrowing slightly.

'Because I thought I'd lose you. That you'd reject me. And I didn't want that to happen,' he said quietly.

'Tell me about Louise.'

'Must I? Do you really want to know?' His eyes were clouded with pain as they looked at her.

'I want to know, Alex.' Emma's voice was dangerously low. 'Do you still love her?'

'How can you ask that?' Anger shadowed his tone. 'Haven't I shown you how much I love you?'

'You've made love to me, Alex, but that doesn't mean anything, does it? Any man could do that.'

'Don't look at me as if you hate me, Emma,' he pleaded. 'I should have told you, I know, but I was terrified I'd lose you if I did.'

'And you have a son.'

He lowered his head.

'Yes, I have a son. I should have told you that too. What can I say? There's no excuse. I've been unfair. But so have you, Emma.'

'Me?' she protested indignantly.

'How long have you known and said nothing?'

She felt her cheeks flood with fire

and couldn't meet his angry, accusing eyes.

'Presumably Henry told you. I guessed he might. But you didn't say a word, and so I thought it didn't matter.'

'Didn't matter! A wife and child, and you thought it didn't matter!' she flared.

'You're the one that matters to me now, Emma. You're the most important person in my life. The most wonderful thing that's ever happened to me. And I love you. I don't know what else to say: except to ask you to forgive me.'

He was looking at her with such anguished appeal in his gaze that Emma couldn't resist any longer. Her arms slipped round his neck, bringing his face down to hers and her mouth parted at his kiss as they sank back into the soft warmth of the bed, their bodies merging once more into one sweet act of forgiveness.

Later that morning, with the car heading west along the motorway, Emma began to feel apprehensive. She was facing a completely new way of life: a marriage, a stepson, a house she'd never known before. As if sensing her anxiety, Alex turned to smile at her, resting his hand on her knee for a second, before concentrating on the drive.

'You'll love it when you get there, darling.'

'Will I?' she said doubtfully.

'Of course you will. It's the most perfect place in the world. And I know you'll love Jamie. Everybody does. He may be a little shy at first, but once he gets to know you . . . '

He paused, before continuing more slowly.

'And then, of course, there's Rachel. She may take a bit more getting used to.'

'Rachel?' The word sprang from her lips. *What else has he been keeping from me?*

'She's been taking care of Jamie. You may find her rather possessive, almost too much so. But then, I really don't know what I'd have done without her. She's been such a great help since . . . '

It's as if he can't bring himself to mention the finality of Louise's death, Emma thought, but why? It's three years. Surely he must be over it by now.

'Jamie started at the village school just after Christmas. He's coping quite well, although his teacher does say he's somewhat withdrawn and finds it hard to mix with the other children. He's quite mature in some ways, but that's from always being in grown-up company, I suppose.'

He leaned sideways to kiss her cheek.

'When we have our own children, I dare say he'll soon change.'

A half-smile quivered round Emma's lips.

'So you intend us to have a family, do you?'

'After last night, I should think it's inevitable, wouldn't you?' he replied with a mischievous grin. 'Why, do you mind?'

'No, but not too soon,' she said. 'I

rather enjoy practising at the moment.'

'Really, Mrs Crawley,' he laughed with a tilt of his eyebrows. 'I didn't realise I'd married a wanton.'

'Then maybe you should have got to know me a little better first.'

'No,' he answered softly. 'Getting to know you is the most exciting part of all.'

They stopped just outside Salisbury for lunch and by late afternoon were skirting Plymouth, then crossing the Tamar bridge into Cornwall.

'How far is it now?' Emma asked, gazing down at the wide expanse of grey water, scattered with boats.

'About another sixty miles I should think.'

'So far?'

Alex smiled back at her.

'Are you getting tired? We could've done it in two stages, but I wanted to get back to Roseland again as soon as possible. I'm dying for you to see the place. It's a lovely part of the coast.'

'Roseland?'

'The Roseland Peninsula. It's across the water from Falmouth, not far from St. Mawes.'

'But I thought you lived in Truro.'

'I only work there. My home's right on the coast near St. Anthony.'

The sun was beginning to sink low, tinting the clouds with flame when they turned down a narrow, high-banked, twisting lane, its lush green banks bright with colour; the delicate pink spikes of foxgloves and drifts of bluebells mingling with the gold of buttercups and white campion. Overhead the trees leaned together forming a cool leafy arch.

Through them, on one side, Emma could catch glimpses of the azure sea. It was like entering another world. She'd never imagined anything so beautiful.

With one final twist, the lane dropped steeply almost to the edge of the sea and Alex stopped the car outside a white-washed cottage, its low roof thatched, scarlet roses climbing the smooth walls, and turned to watch her reaction.

A low grey-stone wall ran along the front, its top covered in purple aubretia with pink and yellow rock roses trailing over and down to the ground, while tubs of late tulips glowed richly on either side of the glass-windowed front door, overhung by a thatched porch.

Laughing at her bemused expression, Alex bent to lift her up and carry her over the threshold, his mouth finding hers as he did so, and lingering in one long kiss.

When Emma drew her flushed face away, she was aware of a chilling silence. Standing at the foot of the stairs, her thin face taut with disapproval, was a gaunt dark-haired woman.

'Emma, this is Rachel,' he said, lowering her quickly to the ground, smoothing down her full-skirted dress as he did so.

The woman made no attempt to greet or even acknowledge her, but fixed her dark gaze on Alex.

'Jamie's asleep. Please don't wake him.'

'Already?'

Emma could see the disappointment in his expression.

'I was hoping you'd keep him up, as it's a special occasion, Rachel.'

Rachel's mouth thinned. 'How could I, seeing as you didn't inform me when you were to be expected? And anyway, the child has a routine. His bedtime is seven o'clock as well you know.'

She must be in her late thirties, or maybe early forties, Emma thought, studying the woman's lined face. Plainly dressed too, in a straight grey skirt and cream paisley printed blouse. No make-up. Her straight dark hair drawn back into a pony tail that looked somewhat out of place on a woman of that age.

Still she chose to ignore Emma, not even glancing in her direction, who began to find it annoying.

'Hullo, Rachel,' she said, determined to make some form of contact. 'I was so looking forward to meeting Jamie too. Could I just go up and peep at him?'

Cold grey eyes met hers. 'No,' Rachel said, 'you couldn't.'

She recoiled at the fierce note in the woman's voice, and Alex touched her arm with a soothing gesture. 'Perhaps later, darling,' he suggested. 'Now, Rachel, we're starving. Is there anything for us to eat?'

'You didn't tell me you'd be wanting a meal,' she retorted.

'Never mind,' Emma interrupted, seeing the anger that was beginning to fill Alex's eyes. 'I'll go into the kitchen and see what I can find. I'm quite good at making meals out of nothing.'

With a quick movement, Rachel stepped in front of her, barring the way.

'I don't like anyone in my kitchen,' she snapped.

'Your kitchen?' Emma queried, meeting the grey eyes without flinching. She saw the flush that darkened the woman's sallow cheeks and knew her words had hit hard.

'We'll go down to 'The Smugglers', darling. They do a good meal there. It'll save a lot of bother,' Alex said quietly, taking her arm. 'It's not far.'

As they walked down the winding street, the last rays of sunshine patterning the cobbles with shadows, Emma turned angrily to him.

'What an extremely unpleasant woman.'

'Don't take any notice of her, darling. I told you Rachel's rather possessive. She'll soon change when she gets used to you.'

'She won't have to bother, will she?'

'What do you mean?' he asked.

'Well, there's no reason for her to stay, now that I'm here.'

Alex gave her a startled look.

'I can't just get rid of her.'

'Why not?'

'She's been here ever since Jamie was born.'

'But I thought Rachel came after Louise's death?'

Alex shook his head.

'No. Louise found it difficult to cope with a baby and she had quite a social life too, so we employed Rachel when Jamie was about three weeks old. She's looked after him ever since.'

He pushed open the low age-darkened wood door of an inn right by the edge of the harbour and guided her inside to a roar of greeting from the group of fishermen crowded round the bar.

'Nice to see you, Alex.'

A thick-set, smooth-haired, deeply tanned, middle-aged man sauntered across the room, hand outstretched.

'So this is the new bride you've been telling us so much about,' he smiled, taking Emma's hands in his and squeezing them with a friendly, rather over-familiar gesture. 'Well, you always did have an eye for a pretty woman, didn't you, Alex?'

Emma noticed her husband's face stiffen at the man's words.

'This is Brian Pendower, Emma. He owns 'The Smugglers'.'

'Be careful how you word it, Alex. You make me sound like a wicked villain in charge of a bunch of cut-throats with that description.'

'A villain?' Alex seemed to linger over the word.

'No, I mustn't call you that, must I, Brian?'

There was a rising tension in the air, the men grouped round the bar watching silently, their drinking stilled. Emma was very aware of the intense dislike that Alex had for the other man, and wondered why. He seemed extremely friendly.

'Is it too late for a meal?' she enquired, hoping to ease the heightening atmosphere.

'For you, my dear, anything is possible,' Brian Pendower smiled, pressing her fingers once more, then led the way to a table in a corner of the dimly-lit room, pulling out a chair and guiding her into it with one lingering hand low on her back.

'I can't stand that man,' Alex

muttered, glowering after him as Brian walked across to the bar and picked up two menus.

'So I noticed.'

'Don't get too friendly with him, Emma. He has quite a reputation round this way — and the morals of a tom-cat.'

Emma raised her eyebrows in amusement.

'I thought he seemed very charming.'

'Women usually do,' Alex retorted drily.

They selected their meal and sat drinking white wine until it came: beautifully tender steaks, with tiny button mushrooms, thick slices of tomato and crisply sautéd potatoes, accompanied by a delicious salad.

Brian Pendower was very attentive, constantly returning to pour more wine into their glasses, his hand lightly brushing Emma's each time he did so. Alex noticed the gesture and Emma could see an angry pulse flicker in his cheek, his mouth drawing into a thin line of annoyance which sent a frisson of excitement pulsing through her when she sensed his jealousy.

It was dark outside when they finally left, weaving somewhat unsteadily up the hill to their cottage, overcome with tiredness and a little too much wine.

The sea lapped gently along the shore and a full moon brightened the night sky, glinting on each breaking wave. A smell of wet seaweed mingled with salt prickled Emma's nostrils, making her want to sneeze, as she clung to Alex's arm for support.

From the tiny gardens of the whitewashed terraced cottages clustered along the roadside came the heavy scent of wallflowers and roses.

Under her feet the cobbles were uneven making Emma cling even more tightly to Alex as her high heels wavered. He drew her closer, pressing her body hard against his, kissing the top of her hair when they reached their front door and he searched for, and found, the lock.

'Do you think Rachel's gone to bed?' Emma whispered.

'I hope so,' he murmured, letting his lips move along the line of her throat to the top of her dress, his fingers undoing the tiny buttons as they crept up the creaking stairs.

Inside their bedroom she turned to him, her body eager for his, feeling the thrill of his naked skin against hers.

'Welcome home, Mrs Crawley,' he whispered, and for one fleeting second she wondered whether he was thinking of Louise, before she found herself moving to an intoxicating rhythmn, and forgot about everything else.

She woke, alone, to sunshine streaming in through the diamond-paned window and the gentle pounding of the sea surrounding the cliffs. Downstairs she could hear the sound of movement and a smell of toast wafted up to her. Quickly she showered.

A murmur of voices came from what she guessed must be the kitchen and she went in to find Alex sitting at the table deep in conversation with a little boy, while Rachel's straight back stiffly turned away towards the grill.

The sight of the child surprised her. She'd imagined Jamie would be a miniature of his father, but although the bright blue eyes were similar, his complexion was very fair and his hair bleached almost white by the sun and sea.

He regarded her solemnly, spoon poised over a bowl of cornflakes.

'This is Emma,' Alex told him. 'She's come to live with us now.'

Jamie continued to stare as if absorbing everything about her and Emma smiled at him, rather nonplussed. Children were something with which she'd had little contact and she wasn't quite sure how to approach him.

'As it's Sunday, I thought we'd take a picnic lunch to the beach,' Alex suggested.

'It's going to be hot, I'm not sure Jamie should spend too long down there,' Rachel informed him, moving swiftly to rest one hand protectively on the child's shoulder. 'You know how easily he burns.'

'We'll sit in the shade then,' said Emma, determined to be included in the conversation.

Rachel eyed her coldly.

'I think I know what's best for the boy,' she observed and Emma flinched at the sharpness in her voice.

'Then I'll have to learn too, won't I, Rachel?' she replied firmly.

The thin fingers tightened on Jamie's shoulder, but the woman said no more, turning back to the stove to pour eggs into a saucepan and beating them furiously.

'Can I do that for you?' Emma enquired.

Rachel's back went rigid and her tone was chilling as she replied, 'No . . . thank you.'

'Perhaps we'd better start eating in the dining-room now we're a proper family,' Alex suggested lightly. 'I'm afraid I usually eat on my own from a tray, while Jamie has his with Rachel earlier. We shall have to become more civilised in future.'

'But it's beautiful in here,' Emma observed. 'Especially with such a fantastic view over the garden and out to sea.'

'So has the dining-room. That's the advantage of overlooking a curving bay. Most of the rooms have a good view.'

'Well, let's have breakfast in here anyway, and leave the dining-room for more formal meals,' she said. 'Will you help me make the picnic, Jamie?'

The small face lit up but before he could answer, Rachel interrupted.

'Jamie will be going to Sunday school at ten o'clock.'

'Well, we'll do it when you come home again, Jamie.'

'I shall have it all ready by then,' retorted Rachel swiftly.

Emma smiled reassuringly at the little boy who was looking from one to the other with anxious eyes.

'Don't worry, I'll wait until you come

back, then we'll get everything ready together.'

'There's no need, Mrs Crawley.' Rachel's voice was determined.

Emma smiled at her sweetly.

'Surely you must have a day off?'

'I don't need a day off.'

'Good gracious me, I didn't realise you were such a tyrant, Alex,' Emma laughed, glancing reprovingly at her husband who was deeply engrossed in the *Sunday Times*. 'Of course you must have time off, Rachel, and we shall start with today. You know what they say about all work and no play.'

She could see the anger darkening the other woman's face and didn't care. No way was she going to be dictated to in what was now her own home. With a furious glare, Rachel caught Jamie's arm and gave it a quick jerk.

'Upstairs and get ready,' she ordered.

Emma bit back her words of protest at the woman's sharpness. At the moment she was only a stranger to them both, but given time she would make her wishes quite clear. She realised that Rachel had been in control of both the child and the house for a long time now. It was going to take a while for her to relinquish the reins and Emma didn't want to upset things by rushing the situation. Even so she hated the manner in which Rachel treated the little boy, and even more the apparent lack of interest that his father took.

'Come on, Alex,' she said, giving the newspaper a shake.

His blue eyes quizzed her in surprise.

'We're taking Jamie to Sunday school.'

'Are we?'

'Don't you usually?' she asked.

Alex shook his head.

'No, Rachel does.'

'Well, today we are. It's Rachel's day off.'

'I've already told Mrs Crawley — ' Rachel began, but Emma cut in quickly.

'Fancy not letting her have any time off, Alex. I'm surprised at you. Right then, Rachel, off you go and don't worry about a thing. I'll get Jamie ready.'

'But — '

'No buts, Rachel. It's a beautiful day. Don't waste it.'

With another sweet smile, Emma quickly left the room and ran up the stairs to Jamie's small bedroom. Inside she could hear muffled movements and gently tapped on the door before going in.

'Nearly ready?' she asked. He nodded.

'Shall I tie your shoe laces for you?'

'I can do that,' he replied indignantly, bending down to show her. 'I am nearly six, you know.'

'Well, Jamie, I'm afraid I don't know a great deal about children. I'm going to have to learn and I'll need a lot of help.'

The little boy stared up at her suspiciously as if uncertain whether she was being serious or not, but she met his gaze with honest eyes.

'Well, next I have to clean my teeth

and then brush my hair,' he informed her. 'But Rachel sometimes has to do that 'cos I get the parting muddled.'

'Shall I then?'

'After my teeth,' he said, opening the door and going into the bathroom.

Emma could hear the rush of water and then a lot of spitting before he returned, smelling strongly of peppermint.

'Have you been eating the toothpaste?' she asked him.

A cheeky smile lit his face.

'Just a tiny bit. Now it's my hair. That's the brush.'

He stood in front of her, bending his head slightly and she began to brush the fine fair hair lightly.

'Rachel does it harder than that to get the tangles out.'

Rachel would, Emma thought grimly.

'I'm not sure that parting's very good. What do you think?' she said.

Jamie studied himself solemnly in the mirror.

'Bit wobbly,' was his comment.

'Shall I try again?'

He nodded and Emma smoothed the fine hair once more, marvelling at its softness. 'Okay?' she asked.

He smiled at her from the mirror. 'Okay.'

'Then let's go and find daddy.'

'Daddy?'

He stopped mid-way down the stairs to look back at her.

'Your daddy and I are going to take you this morning.'

'Not Rachel?'

'I've decided it's her day off.'

'She never does usually.'

'Well Jamie, don't forget I'm learning how to look after you now, so I have to practise.'

'Will it take long?' he asked.

'It depends on how well you teach me.'

'Me?'

'You. How else am I going to learn?'

'Then what?'

'We shan't need Rachel any more.'

Emma was aware of a sudden

tenseness in the air surrounding them.

Rachel stood in the hallway near the front door, her thin face pale, gazing up at her with blazing eyes.

# 3

'Just off, Rachel?' Emma smiled. 'Well, have a lovely day, won't you.'

With a loud bang, the door slammed forcefully.

'Ready, Alex?'

There was a rustle of papers from the lounge and Alex appeared, shrugging his shoulders into a pale cream suede jacket.

'You do realise you're causing total disruption to my household?' he grinned, bending to kiss her.

'As if I would,' she smiled back.

'Poor Rachel, packed off for the day, and you taking over her duties.'

'Do you mind? Isn't that what I'm here for?'

'Not quite all,' he replied with a mischievous wink.

'It's nearly ten o'clock,' Jamie interrupted importantly. 'That's the church bell.'

'Is it very far?' Emma asked.

'Up the hill,' Jamie told her, catching her hand and tugging her towards the door. 'Hurry or I'll be late. Will you and daddy come to meet me too?'

'Of course we will,' she replied and saw the wide smile of pleasure that spread over his upturned face. 'Doesn't Rachel?'

'Yes, but that's different.'

At the door of the church hall, Jamie stopped and stood hesitantly looking at Emma, who quickly bent her head and was rewarded by the warm moist brush of his lips against her cheek.

'You will be there, won't you?' he asked, blue eyes wide and questioning.

'Of course we will, Jamie,' she answered.

'So what are we going to do for the next hour in an empty house all by ourselves?' Alex enquired with a quizzical look.

'I could prepare the picnic,' Emma suggested innocently.

'I thought you promised that Jamie

could help,' he reminded her.

'So I did,' she smiled. 'Well, it's back to the Sunday papers then.'

'That's what you think,' he laughed, his arm tightening round her waist as they walked back down the hill.

'What d'you think Rachel will do with herself all day? Has she any family?' Emma asked later, sinking back into the smooth pillows of their bed.

'Her mother's still alive. Rachel visits her quite a lot; she often takes Jamie with her. She has a cottage down near the harbour. And there's a sister on the Lizard, I believe. I don't really know a great deal about her.'

'Really, Alex! The woman's lived here for nearly six years and you don't know a great deal about her. What an admission!'

'She's not exactly my type, darling,' he said, idly teasing her nipple with one finger.

'For all you know she's probably been madly in love with you all these years, and now that I've appeared, feels terribly thwarted.'

'Don't be ridiculous!'

'Just because you don't fancy her, doesn't mean it's mutual. I should imagine every woman you meet is drawn under your spell, like I am,' she murmured, conscious of the desire he was arousing in her heated body once more.

'Come on, you wanton. Get dressed, because if you lay there any longer looking like that, we're going to be very late collecting Jamie.'

★  ★  ★

'Now then, what shall we take with us for the picnic, Jamie?' Emma asked as they stood in the kitchen, surveying the contents of the larder and fridge.

'Paste sandwiches.'

'Paste sandwiches! That's a bit boring, isn't it?'

'Rachel always makes paste sandwiches for a picnic.'

'Then we'll have something different.

You wash those tomatoes and the cucumber for me while I shred this lettuce and we'll make a salad. I'll cut some slices of this cold chicken. Can you pull three bananas off that bunch and we'll take those too. And some apples. Oh, and there's a french loaf. That'll be lovely if I chop it down the middle and fill it with the salad.'

She stood Jamie on a chair by the sink and left him with a bowl of water, tearing off yards of kitchen paper to dry the tomatoes.

'We'd better have some plates. Are there any old ones, Jamie?'

With a last slosh of water, he dried his hands and climbed down from the chair, opening one of the long cupboards lining the walls. Emma selected three brightly coloured plates and put them in the basket.

'Now something to drink,' she said, looking in the fridge again.

'There's squash. We could put it in that nearly empty bottle,' Jamie suggested.

'And some wine for daddy.'

'That's in the larder. Under that shelf,' Jamie told her, rushing across and pointing.

'Okay then, we're ready. Go and tell daddy, will you.'

With a scamper of feet the little boy ran off and Emma tucked a red check tablecloth into the basket with some paper serviettes, then carried it all into the hall.

'He's asleep!' Jamie whispered, meeting her on tiptoe.

'Then we'll have to wake him up,' Emma laughed, twitching aside the newspaper and looking down at her husband's handsome tanned face, letting out a shriek of alarm as he seized her round the waist and kissed her.

'He was pretending all the time,' Jamie announced, watching them warily.

'Come on, lazy bones, off to the beach.'

'We'll go through the garden and over the field. There's a path down from there,' said Alex, picking Jamie up and perching him on his shoulders. 'Can you manage the basket?'

'And the rug,' laughed Emma.

'And my bucket and spade,' reminded Jamie.

'I can't see Rachel doing all this,' Emma declared, tucking the rug under one arm while Alex closed the door behind them. At the end of the small garden was a gate half-hidden in the thick hedge.

'This is quite a picture late in the summer,' Alex told her. 'Fuchsia. It grows like wild round here and gets covered in flowers from about August onwards.'

They made their way through the waist-high fronds of grass, Jamie clinging tightly to his father's broad forehead with clutching fingers, his face glowing with happiness.

'Which way now?' enquired Emma when they reached the narrow track running along the cliff-top.

'That way,' Jamie insisted, pointing

sideways. 'There's some steps.'

In the shelter of the cliff, the sun was warm and Emma stretched herself on the rug, while Jamie and Alex built a very large and complicated castle.

'So that's what civil engineering does for you,' she teased. 'Is this where you do all your practising?'

In answer Alex began to cover her feet with sand, encouraging Jamie to do the same, but the little boy stood watching with alarmed blue eyes, hearing her shrieks of protest.

'Don't hurt her!' he shouted, swinging his spade round and hitting Alex sharply across the legs, raising a thin line of blood.

'You little demon!' his father roared angrily, making a grab at him but Jamie darted out of his reach and then stood quite still, as if transfixed, staring out into the bay.

Emma followed his gaze to where someone was swimming, a brilliant peacock-blue cap showing bright against the smooth water.

'It's mummy! It's mummy!' Jamie shrieked, and Emma saw Alex's face go pale under his tan, his eyes sharp with horror, watching the swimmer disappear behind the rocks leading into the next cove.

Emma quickly slipped her arm round the little boy's quivering shoulders and gave him a hug.

'No, Jamie, it's not mummy.'

'It is, it is,' he insisted, his small face pleading.

Alex was gathering up the basket and rug.

'What are you doing?' questioned Emma.

'Going back to the house.'

'But why? We've only just come down here,' she protested.

'We can't stay . . . now.'

'Why ever not? You're being ridiculous, Alex. Just because you saw someone swimming . . . '

He gazed past her almost as if she wasn't there, then said reluctantly, 'Yes, I suppose I am,' and began to lay the rug back down on the sand again.

Emma squeezed his arm lightly.

'I'm sorry if Jamie upset you, Alex.'

But it was as if the sun had gone behind a cloud for the rest of the afternoon. Alex sat, staring out to sea all the time and Jamie was restless and still obviously distressed. Emma did all she could to distract him, taking his hand and going down to the water's edge to collect shells, but he pulled away from her with a frown and went to sit next to his father, leaning his small fair head against him.

When she set out the lunch, they both picked at it and in the end the seagulls ate far more than anyone.

Clouds were beginning to gather, piling up thick and dark over the sea, a chill wind creeping in, blowing the sand in thin swirls across the flatness of the beach.

With a sigh, Emma gathered everything together again and they all trudged back to the house, leaving a trail of damp sand over the kitchen floor as they went in.

I'd better sweep that away before Rachel gets home, Emma thought, searching for a dustpan and brush in one of the cupboards, but Rachel had already returned and appeared, her face stiff and tight, tut-tutting with annoyance.

'Did you have a nice day?' Emma enquired, startled by her sudden entry into the kitchen. 'Where did you go?'

'I visited my mother,' came the curt answer.

'Perhaps I could meet her one day?'

Rachel's slate-like eyes snapped at her.

'Mother doesn't take kindly to strangers. Now, if you'd like to move out of the way, I'll set about clearing up all this mess.'

★ ★ ★

'Can Emma read me a story?' Jamie pleaded when it was time for him to go to bed.

64

'What about me?' his father asked. 'I thought I was the story-teller.'

'Emma's different.' He tugged at her hand. 'Please, Emma.'

'Only if you're bathed and in bed in ten minutes,' said Emma.

'You bath me then 'cos there isn't a clock in the bathroom.'

Jamie gave Rachel sidelong look.

'And it is Rachel's day off, isn't it?'

Oh dear, thought Emma, eyeing her warily, now I'll be in worse trouble, but Rachel merely raised her chin in the air and said, 'If I'm not wanted, then I'll be off to church, and pop in afterwards to see how Mother's getting on. She's been a bit peaky lately — arthritis, you know.'

Surprised at such a wealth of unexpected information, Emma smiled at her and said that would be fine, then hurried up the stairs with the little boy eagerly leading the way.

Alex put his head round the bathroom door minutes later when shrieks of laughter made him curious, to find them blowing bubbles with a cup of washing-up liquid, their hair misted with rainbows of soapy water.

By the time he'd joined in and been shown how to make a circle with his thumb and forefinger to blow a perfect bubble, the ten minutes had stretched into nearly half an hour.

'Can I still have a story, Emma?' Jamie asked when at last he was tucked up under the covers, his hair brushed dry again.

'I promised, didn't I?' she said.

'Yes, but the clock's gone a long way past bedtime now.'

'Never mind.'

'Won't Rachel be cross?'

Emma shook her head. 'Of course she won't.'

'I like you being here, Emma,' Jamie smiled, snuggling down into the covers.

'And so do I,' she smiled back at him, bending to kiss the flushed cheek he offered, then gave a little gasp of surprise as his arms came up and hugged her.

'I can see I've a rival for your affections,' Alex remarked from where he'd been standing behind her in the doorway, watching them.

'Jealous?' she asked.

'So long as it's only a six-year-old,' he grinned. 'Anything older and I'd soon change my views.'

★  ★  ★

'Shall we go down on the beach again today, Jamie?' Emma asked him while they all ate breakfast in the kitchen next morning.

'Jamie will be at school,' Rachel put in quickly.

'Oh yes, so you will, I was forgetting. Maybe afterwards then, Jamie?' she said, turning back to the child.

'We'll see,' replied Rachel and avoided Emma's questioning glance.

'I'll take him to school, Rachel.'

'That won't be necessary, Mrs Crawley. I have shopping to do in the village,' came the swift retort.

'I want Emma to take me, not you, Rachel,' Jamie protested.

'You'll do as you're told, young man,' snapped Rachel, giving him a shake.

Emma could see tears welling in the child's eyes and felt a wave of anger, but before she could speak Alex gave her a warning glance and said quietly, 'Rachel will take you, Jamie. She's going down to the village in any case. Now stop grizzling like a baby and get ready or you'll be late.'

'Really, Alex, how can you be so unfair?' Emma stormed at him when the little boy and Rachel had gone upstairs. 'How on earth am I supposed to get to know Jamie if Rachel butts in all the time?'

'It's you that's being unfair, darling. You must learn to take things gradually. Don't forget that Rachel's been looking after Jamie for most of his life. We can't just cut her out of it like that. Why don't you try to work together for a while. In time we can make the break, but not for a while yet.'

He chuckled at the sight of Emma's face.

'Come on now, darling. You're pouting just like Jamie does when he can't get his own way. Don't be too hard on poor old Rachel. After all, Jamie's been her whole life up till now.'

Emma gave a wry smile.

'I suppose I am being a bit childish, aren't I? But, Alex, I do so want to be a proper mother to him, the same as I'm trying to be a proper wife to you. You've both missed out on a lot in recent years and I want to make it up to you.'

'Well, I can assure you you're succeeding very well,' he laughed, 'but don't rush things too much with Rachel. She'll come round in the end. I'm quite sure she's not as terrible as you like to make out.'

A wave of hot colour flushed over Emma's cheeks at the accusation.

'I'm only going on what I've seen so far, Alex,' she retorted sharply. 'I can't exactly say she acts very lovingly towards Jamie and he's so full of affection himself.'

'He gets that from his father,' Alex grinned wickedly, lifting up her indignant chin and kissing her firmly on the lips before she could raise any more protests. 'Now, I'm off to work so for goodness sake keep the peace while I'm away.'

'Anyone would think I was making all the fuss,' Emma observed crossly.

'Well . . . '

★   ★   ★

What on earth am I going to do with myself all day? Emma wondered miserably as she stood, waving goodbye, watching his car disappear round the first twist in the lane. The thought hadn't occurred to her before and now the time loomed ominously with only Rachel for company.

The breakfast washing-up had already been done and stacked carefully away by Rachel, who was coming down the stairs with a neat and tidy Jamie by her side.

'You look smart,' Emma commented, bending to kiss him goodbye.

'I hate socks,' the little boy muttered, vigorously scratching his leg.

'Never mind, when you come home this afternoon, we'll go paddling,' she comforted and was rewarded by a glower from Rachel.

'I could walk down with you,' Emma suggested tentatively.

'One of us is quite enough, Mrs Crawley. We don't want to get him too excited when he has a day's schooling ahead of him, do we?'

Emma could only agree and stood waving as they walked down the hill, with Jamie turning round every so often and being jerked on again by Rachel's impatient hand until she decided it was kinder to go indoors and let him make the journey untroubled.

Once they were gone, and she knew she had the house to herself, Emma set about exploring every room, feeling extremely guilty as she did so.

It *is* my house, after all, she told herself, so why shouldn't I see what's what?

The cottage was quite large and she decided it must have been a terrace of at least three, converted into one many years before. The lounge ran the whole depth from front to back, overlooking the lane on one side and the pretty garden from the other, with sea views glinting through every window.

She admired the plain white walls hung with watercolours in light-coloured frames of what she presumed were the local area: delicate seascapes and sweeps of moorland and cliff, some quite large and others only tiny miniatures.

The curtains and furnishings were all of chintz with a hazy pattern of flowers in deep blues and greens that toned with the pale grey-blue carpet on the floor, surrounded by a border of polished wooden parquet.

The hall was shadowy and quite

narrow, almost a corridor, with a wide staircase rising at one end turning sharply at right angles half-way to the upper landing where a long window stretched its length. Old and faded Persian rugs covered the gleaming polished boards that creaked with every footstep. Against one wall a grandfather clock ticked away the minutes with solemn dignity and melodically chimed each quarter.

A huge bow window made the dining-room very light and airy, looking out over the lawn where croquet hoops were stuck into the smooth grass and a white painted summer-house stood at one end, waiting for the long warm days to come.

Inside the room a dark walnut table glistened with a deep shine and the six chairs around it had seats of a rich wine-red damask that complemented the jewel-bright colours of the Persian carpet covering the floor. On the long sideboard a pair of silver candelabra shone and a small cut-glass bowl of early roses stood, reflecting back, filling the air with their faint scent.

Halfway between the lounge and dining-room was another door and opening it Emma found she was in Alex's study, meticulously neat and tidy, with an enormous old-fashioned desk and shelves full of textbooks and bound volumes of journals.

Climbing the stairs Emma paused. At one end of the landing she knew was Rachel's bedroom and although greatly tempted to open the door and peep inside, she managed to restrain herself and opened Jamie's instead, to tidy up and make his bed.

The small room was almost spartan. Again, as with the rest of the cottage, plain white walls greeted her, but unadorned with not even a fairy-tale or television character to brighten them. A low chest of drawers with a mirror that he could just see into was placed under the window, while a heavy oak wardrobe stood, dark and forbidding, almost filling one wall. His bed was narrow and old-fashioned with a thickly carved wooden headboard, and covered by a flowered eiderdown.

Not a child's room at all. Merely a hotch-potch of things that must have been in the cottage for years, thought Emma, and she resolved to do something about it the next weekend when they could all go into Truro or Falmouth.

Their own bedroom she also resolved to change. At the moment she could feel Louise's influence everywhere. The neat twin beds carefully covered in oyster-coloured silk bedspreads, to match the curtains. The white-wood dressing-table skirted with the same silken material and topped by three mirrors that emphasised the feminity of its previous owner. Even the walls were pretentious, panelled with long wardrobe fitments, mirror-fronted to reflect every movement in the sugar-sweet room.

Emma found it embarrassing, seeing herself from every angle, wherever she looked. To some women it might have been facinating, but not to her.

She was surprised that Alex had kept the room as it was, until she opened the remaining door and found a fourth bedroom, so obviously masculine that she realised this was where he usually slept.

A trip to one of the larger towns was definitely a must, she decided, and the sooner the better. Maybe she could drive in during the week and have a browse round, so that they could make a final decision together on Saturday.

With a guilty start she heard the front door slam and heard footsteps climbing the stairs. Quickly she came out of the room and closed it quietly, meeting Rachel on the landing.

'Prying, Mrs Crawley?'

'No, Rachel,' she replied, feeling her cheeks flare at the implied insult as the woman's grey eyes quickly flickered towards her own bedroom door. 'But I don't think I have to explain my actions in my own house.'

She saw from the way Rachel's mouth tightened that the remark had hit home.

'I keep forgetting, Mrs Crawley, that you live here now. It was all rather sudden, you see. But then, Alex always is rather unpredictable when it comes to his choice of wife. Unfortunately he seems to pick the wrong one every time.'

She brushed past Emma and opened the door of her room and in the brief glimpse that she could see, a strange brightness glared out. Surely the walls couldn't be red?

Downstairs in the kitchen she made some coffee and put it on a little tray. When Rachel came back down, Emma smiled and poured a cup, passing it across the table.

For a second Rachel seemed taken aback, staring at it doubtfully.

'You do drink coffee, don't you?' enquired Emma, passing her the sugar bowl. 'Look, Rachel, please let's be friends. I know it must be pretty dreadful for you to have me suddenly thrust upon you, but for Jamie's sake we should get on, you know.'

She could see the other woman's lips working together, pursing, then relaxing slightly into what was almost a smile.

'I'm sorry if it all came as rather a shock, but these things happen sometimes. Alex and I fell in love, and that was that. There was no way we could stay apart.'

Rachel's small eyes narrowed slightly.

'You're not a bit like the first Mrs Crawley,' she observed. 'I'm surprised he even noticed you, after her.'

'Tell me about her, Rachel. I need to know.'

'Louise was beautiful.'

Her voice took on a sharp, harsh note, rising slightly as she continued. 'Long blonde hair, so fine it was like gossamer. Skin like a peach. And a body like a goddess — even after the baby. If you'd seen her down on the beach . . . She was unforgettable. Every man thought so.'

Then, with a look of total bitterness, she turned her gaze to Emma.

'And Alex worshipped her. No one else can ever take her place in his heart.'

Once again Emma remembered their wedding night and the word Alex had murmured so longingly.

# 4

Emma quickly realised that there was no way Rachel was going to let her do anything to help in the house, so after a while she pulled on a jumper over her T-shirt and jeans and went out through the garden to the cliff path.

It was a clear, bright morning, the sea a dark shade of blue flecked with tiny waves that ruffled its smooth surface as she stood looking down, the wind blowing her red-gold hair round her cheeks. Taking the opposite direction to the beach this time, she found the tumbled earth and lumps of rock of a landslip, where a track led down to the smoothness of the sand.

For May the sun was surprisingly warm and she tugged off her sandals to walk along the water's edge, enjoying its coolness, her thoughts running back over the past days.

A month ago none of this existed for her. A month ago she'd never even met Alex. Now she was married to him and starting a completely new life — with the home and child created by another woman.

Louise.

If I'd known about her, would I still be here? she wondered. And yet why should it make any difference? Louise had been dead for three years. It was a long time.

But she knew from the way he'd reacted yesterday on the beach that Alex hadn't forgotten her. A woman swimming in the bay. But why should it have such a shattering impact?

A frond of seaweed brushed her foot and Emma bent to pick it up. It was fine and feathery, reddish brown like a mermaid's hair clinging round her fingers.

Louise had drowned. Was it here in this peaceful little cove? She tried to imagine how it would look in a gale, with a sea rising high, thundering against the steep cliffs. But Louise wouldn't have been swimming then, would she?

So why had she died?

The voice behind her made her jump. 'Good morning, Emma.'

Startled, she turned to find Brian Pendower standing there, lean and bronzed wearing only a pair of brief navy shorts that clung to his hard muscular thighs, his sleek grey hair ruffled by the slight sea-breeze as he smiled at her.

'You frightened me,' she confessed.

He reached out to smooth her arm. 'My apologies. I wouldn't want to do that, but you were quite obviously deep in thought. Troubled ones by the expression on your face. What's wrong?'

He fell into step close beside her, still holding her arm, and she was conscious of the warmth of his skin brushing against hers as they walked.

'It's nothing,' she answered quickly.

With an abrupt movement, he stopped, spinning her round to face him. 'Be honest with me, Emma. You're beginning to have doubts, aren't you?'

'Of course not,' she protested weakly.

'Marry in haste, repent at leisure. Isn't that what they say? And you certainly married in haste, didn't you? Was that the only way Alex could get you into bed with him?'

Emma pulled her arm away from his, glaring furiously into his challenging eyes. 'No it wasn't!' she blazed.

'You went quite willingly then?'

'Alex and I fell in love.'

'Really, Emma! In this day and age! Do you really expect me to believe that? But then, I realise Alex does suffer with a conscience. And he's full of old-fashioned, out-dated morals too, so being such an honourable man, I suppose he would have to marry you.'

'It wasn't like that at all. It was a case of love at first sight, however strange that must sound to you.'

Brian arched his eyebrows to study her face carefully.

'Do you know, Emma, I really think I

have to believe you. It's just the kind of thing Alex would do — and having met you, I can see why. You're quite the most delightfully innocent young maiden I've ever had the good fortune to meet.'

Emma started to walk angrily away and he followed.

'Don't let's fall out,' he pleaded. 'In a small community like this one, you're going to need a friend. It's taken me about twenty years to become accepted, so you've got a long way to go yet. Please, Emma, say you forgive me.'

There was such an air of appeal about him that Emma couldn't resist smiling, and he smiled back, catching her arm once more and tucking it through his.

'That's more like it. Now, tell me honestly, what was making you look so despondent?'

'Louise,' she blurted out.

'Ah, so that's it — being a second wife.'

'That doesn't matter too much, but

84

Louise does. She sounds so fantastic, I'm not sure I can compete.'

'Do you have to?' he asked.

'Alex was married to her . . . and I'm sure he still loves her.'

Brian gave a hoot of laughter.

'My dear child! So you think you're competing with a beautiful ghost. Is that what's worrying you?'

His eyes travelled over her from head to toe in a way that made her face burn.

'Well, from what I can guess is hidden under that rather unglamorous jumper and jeans, I don't think you have any need to get upset.'

His arm tightened on hers, drawing her closer to his tanned body.

'You're here in flesh and blood, Emma, and what man could resist that?'

'But, don't you see, Brian, that makes it even worse. All Alex has is a memory of Louise. The good things about her. And I'm constantly doing and saying everything wrong all the time.'

'I can see why he couldn't resist you,

Emma,' Brian observed, stroking the soft skin of her wrist. 'You're so totally naïve and innocent. Positively enchanting.'

'Oh, Brian! Be serious,' she implored.

'But I am being serious. I've never been more serious in my life.'

'So what do I do? How do I fight back? You knew Louise, didn't you? What was she like? All I know is that she was beautiful.'

'Oh yes,' he replied slowly. 'I knew Louise.'

A wry smile curved his lips.

'Louise was the most beautiful woman I, or any other man for that matter, could ever hope to meet, and she knew it and used it to her advantage. One smile, one upward tilt of a shoulder, one pout of her sensuous lips, and they'd be falling at her feet. She was absolutely gorgeous.'

'Well, that's very comforting for a start,' Emma observed drily.

'Who wants to be married to a woman like that?' he questioned. 'It isn't the basis for contentment, is it? Alex certainly had his problems with Louise — and he was as jealous as hell.'

They'd reached an outcrop of rock now, where the tide swept in, cutting off the rest of the beach. Emma hesitated, ready to turn and walk back, but Brian pulled her down beside him onto a smooth lump of granite to continue their conversation.

'Alex has a ferocious temper, Emma. Be careful not to upset him. He's like a lion when roused.'

'Do you think they were happy?'

'How does one tell? I saw them together enough times, but it's once the bedroom door's closed that the real truth is known about a marriage, isn't it?'

Emma blushed under his quizzical gaze.

'I'm quite sure he won't have any problems with you,' he smiled, patting her knee. 'Now, we'd better be going back. The inn can't manage without me for very long unfortunately.'

He paused and gave her a thoughtful look.

'What do you intend to do with yourself all day?'

'Heaven knows,' she shrugged. 'Rachel seems to be in full command of the house and Jamie's at school. It's going to get a bit boring. You see I had quite an exacting secretarial job in London, so having time on my hands is something new.'

'Come and work for me,' he suggested.

'You?'

'I could do with some help. We have several guests staying during the summer months and it gets somewhat frantic at times.'

'Do you mean as a barmaid?' Emma's voice was full of doubt.

He let out a bellow of laughter.

'A barmaid! Somehow I don't quite see you pulling pints, my dear. No, what I have in mind is the reception side of things, taking bookings, typing letters, doing the accounts, that sort of thing. Does it have any appeal? I realise it's not as enthralling as the work you're probably used to, but it could ward off some of that boredom a little.'

'Can I think about it?'

'Don't leave it too long, will you? I need someone soon.'

He squeezed her hand as they turned to climb back up the beach towards the harbour.

'And maybe it would take your mind off those brooding thoughts too. Pop in any time you like and have a look round the place. It'll give you some idea of what's involved; and I'll always be delighted to see you.'

Emma's thoughts were in a whirl for the rest of the day. She wasn't too sure about Brian's manner and remembered Alex's warning about not letting him get too familiar with her. The morals of a tom-cat, wasn't that what he'd said?

A faint smile curled her mouth.

But Alex was a jealous man, Brian had said, so maybe he'd be like that about anyone who showed the slightest interest in her.

A job would be a good idea and unless she travelled into one of the larger towns, not easy to find locally. Yes, she thought, Brian's offer was definitely worth considering.

★ ★ ★

'I'll go down to meet Jamie,' she told Rachel after lunch and saw the other woman's face grow tight at the suggestion.

'There's no need . . . '

'Look, Rachel, I want to get to know my new stepson and to be honest, with you around all the time, there's not a great deal of opportunity.'

Maybe I'm putting it too bluntly, she thought, but with Rachel there was no other way. She seemed determined to be as obstinate as she could.

'And then I'll take him down onto the beach.'

'What about his tea? The boy's used

to a routine, Mrs Crawley. It isn't fair of you to try and disturb that.'

'We'll have it on the beach. He's such a pale little chap considering he lives right next to the sea. It'll do him good to get some sunshine.'

'He burns easily,' Rachel protested.

'Then I'll buy some suntan cream.'

She saw the woman's look of resignation and gave a sigh of relief.

'If you like to get some tea ready for us while I'm collecting him, then we can go straight down there — and you do know best what he likes to eat, don't you, Rachel?' she added winningly.

Waiting outside the iron railings, Emma studied the other mothers collecting their children — a noisy chattering group who fell silent when she appeared, regarding her suspiciously.

She smiled. 'I'm Emma Crawley,' she said to the nearest woman who was leaning over a pushchair, wiping the nose of a wailing baby.

The woman straightened. 'I know,' she replied abruptly, and turned away to continue her conversation with the long-haired girl standing next to her.

Emma felt rebuffed and remembered Brian's words, but if she was going to live here, she needed to be part of the community too. Perhaps if she invited some of them to tea, after school one day . . .

There was a sudden hubbub of noise and about a dozen children erupted from the opened door, scattering over the grey tarmac of the playground and rushing to the gate.

With anxious eyes, Emma scanned the eager faces for Jamie as they streamed through, clutching at their mothers, thrusting crumpled paintings and other treasures into waiting, outstretched hands, before trailing away along the street, leaving behind a drift of excited chatter.

Emma stood there, growing more worried. Surely she hadn't missed him.

Eventually, when everyone else had

gone and the playground was silent again, she went through the gate and opened the door to find Jamie and a plump, placid-faced, elderly, white-haired lady deep in conversation together.

His face broke into a smile of welcome when he saw her.

'That's Emma, Mrs Trissick,' he explained, turning back to the teacher.

'Ah, Mrs Crawley. I've been hearing a great deal about you from Jamie today,' she smiled, holding out a chalk-whitened hand.

'Oh dear, that sounds ominous.'

'Not at all, my dear. It seems to me you've made a great impression — and a favourable one too, if I may say so. Jamie's usually quite reticent in class, but today he actually stood up when it came to our news-time and told us all about you.'

She turned back to the child and said, 'Would you put all the bean bags away in the cupboard for me please, Jamie,' and when he was safely on the other side of the room, continued her conversation quietly with Emma.

'He's a funny little chap, you know. Quite worrying at times. What with all the trauma in his life, he hasn't found it easy to fit in. He's extremely bright for his age and quite outpaces the rest of the class, but there's no way I can put him up a year until he's learned to adjust properly.'

With careful fingers she was sorting thick wax crayons into a box as she spoke, putting them in straight neat rows.

'He'd far rather spend his day chatting to me, than the other children, and I must say that with such an intelligent child, it's a joy to do so, but not the right way to go about things, I'm afraid.'

Giving Emma a straight look, she remarked firmly, 'Maybe with a settled home life, he'll be much happier though.'

'I hope so, Mrs Trissick,' Emma replied. 'It's what I want more than anything.'

'Trelissick, my dear,' the teacher smiled. 'That's something else we've got to get right with Jamie.'

When he came back to his desk, the little boy picked up a large sheet of paper and held it out shyly.

'I painted that, Emma,' he said, looking up at her with eager blue eyes. 'It's a picture of you.'

Emma studied the splodges of colour, picking out the straight stick-like pink legs and arms, the blue triangular body and round head with its black dots for eyes and curving wide red mouth.

'I did you smiling because you always are,' he explained, watching her face intently.

'It's a lovely picture. The best I've ever seen of me,' she said, catching the thoughtful scrutiny in Mrs Trelissick's gaze. 'We'll put it on the wall in the kitchen when we get back home again.'

'Rachel won't let you,' he told her gravely. 'It's clutter.'

'It's going on the wall, don't you

worry,' Emma replied in a positive tone, taking his hand.

'I can see things are going to change quite dramatically,' Mrs Trelissick smiled as she walked to the school gate with them. 'Goodbye, Mrs Crawley. Goodbye, Jamie.'

★   ★   ★

'Let's explore a bit further along the beach today, Jamie. If we climb down along there where the cliff's fallen away, we can reach a lovely bit of sand. I went that way this morning.'

The little boy looked at her strangely, the long grass waving above his fair head as he stood quite still.

'Come on then,' she encouraged.

'I mustn't.'

His small face was set like a taut mask.

'Because it's crumbling?' she asked him. 'It's all right, Jamie. You'll be quite safe with me. It's not dangerous.'

'I mustn't go any further.'

He stood in the middle of the path, his feet planted firmly.

'Did Rachel say so?'

It would be just like her to make stupid rules like that, Emma thought.

Jamie shook his head.

'Who said you mustn't go any further then?'

'Mummy did.'

'Mummy?'

Emma stared at him incredulously. Three years ago — and he still obeyed?

'Mummy said I must stay here and not go any further,' he repeated obstinately.

'But why?'

He raised his clear blue gaze, so like his father's, to hers.

'Stay there and wait for me to come back, and don't move. That's what she said.'

'Where did mummy go, Jamie?'

'Down on the beach. That's where the caves are.'

'Yes, I know, I saw them this morning.'

She looked at the little boy again. It was quite obvious that he wasn't going any further, whatever she said, so with a smile of encouragement, she turned and went back the other way along the path.

'Okay then, we'll go down the steps.'

Perhaps Louise was only being sensible. Perhaps the cliff had been far more dangerous in the those days and the well-worn track to the beach unsafe.

Cheerfully Jamie trotted along, following happily now, and hand in hand they climbed down the wooden steps to the sand.

It was strange though, Emma thought. Why did Louise take Jamie with her at all if she was only going to leave him alone right at the edge of a dangerous cliff?

'Take off your shoes, Jamie, and put them on the corners of the rug,' she instructed, when the breeze began to lift the edges while she tried to spread it on the ground.

'And you,' he said, running to hold

the other corner down.

'Now, let's see what nice things Rachel's made for our tea,' she said, opening the plastic boxes.

'Paste sandwiches,' Jamie told her, pulling one apart and peering inside.

'I should have known,' she laughed, scrunching grittily into one. 'You did warn me, didn't you?'

They were intent on building a castle when Rachel came down the steps, her face like a thunder-cloud.

'It's half-past six,' she said pointedly, glaring at Emma.

'Already?'

'And Jamie's bedtime is seven o'clock.'

'We've nearly finished,' Jamie smiled up at her, carefully patting out another bucketful of sand and pressing it into place.

'I said it's bedtime,' Rachel observed firmly.

'Five minutes,' Emma said. 'Then we'll be finished.'

Rachel caught Jamie's hand and jerked him roughly to his feet.

'You'll do as you're told, young man,' she snapped.

'Let him finish it, Rachel,' Emma said in a quiet voice. 'He's spent such a long time. It's a beautiful castle, isn't it, Jamie?'

'The boy will do as he's told, Mrs Crawley. Please don't encourage him to be disobedient,' and with one sweeping movement of her foot, Rachel knocked over the neatly built walls, stamping the sand flat again, while Emma stared at her in speechless indignation, hardly believing what she was seeing.

With a muffled sob, Jamie's cold sandy hand crept into hers and she squeezed it sympathetically, watching the tears that rolled silently down his cheeks.

She saw the look that Rachel flashed at her, her thin face full of triumph as she strode back to the steps, leaving them to trail miserably behind her, clutching the damp rug and picnic basket.

★   ★   ★

'She really enjoyed knocking down that castle, Alex,' Emma told him later that evening. 'Poor little mite. He was so upset.'

'Well, you do know what a stickler Rachel is for her routine, darling,' he replied.

'Five minutes, that's all it would've taken. That woman can't bear to see anyone happy.'

'You really don't like her, do you, darling?'

Emma shook her head emphatically. 'I haven't exactly seen much to like yet.'

'Rachel's been extremely good with Jamie, you know. I don't know how I'd have coped without her,' Alex reminded her gently.

'Really, Alex! You haven't the faintest idea, have you? Just because the child is fed and kept clean, you think he's happy, don't you? She's a dragon.'

'Look, Emma,' he said stiffly. 'Don't start upsetting things. It's all very well for you to have bright ideas about what to do, but Jamie's used to a certain way of life and changing it suddenly won't do any good at all.'

'You infuriate me at times, Alex. Don't you care about your son? Rachel's a vicious woman and the sooner she goes, the better.'

'Emma!' he broke in angrily. 'I've told you before. You mustn't rush the situation. It's going to take time for everyone to adjust. Now calm down. Your own attitude isn't good for Jamie either. You're deliberately going out of your way to encourage disobedience.'

Emma looked at him sharply. 'Have you been talking to Rachel?'

Alex met her eyes firmly. 'Yes, she did have a word with me when you were bathing Jamie, and I can see her point too.'

With a determined thrust of her chin, Emma left the room and went to look for Rachel but the kitchen was empty, everything neatly cleared away.

'She's probably gone down to visit

her mother,' Alex said, following closely behind her.

'And complain about me to her as well, I suppose,' Emma raged.

'You're beautiful when you're angry,' Alex teased, kissing the nape of her neck.

'I hate you!'

'Prove it,' he whispered, subtly sliding his hands down her back and moving them slowly round her waist and up to cup her breasts, his mouth closing over hers, preventing any other protest.

★ ★ ★

'I forgot to tell you that I met Brian on the beach yesterday morning. He's offered me a job,' Emma said as she kissed Alex goodbye the following day.

'He did what?'

She wasn't prepared for the blaze of anger that flashed in his blue eyes. 'Offered me a job — as receptionist at the inn.'

'The bloody swine!'

'Alex!' she protested. 'I thought it was rather nice of him.'

'You'll keep away from that man, Emma.'

She stared back at him coldly.

'Are you asking me to do so, Alex?'

'No,' he replied hotly. 'Not asking. Telling you, Emma.'

'I don't take orders, Alex, not even from you.'

'Well, this time you will,' he said, gripping her arm.

She glanced down at his fingers, seeing the whiteness of the knuckles as they held her, and thrust out her chin.

'You're hurting my arm.'

Slowly his hand relaxed and moved away.

Emma studied the line of red marks outlined on her skin and raised her eyes to his, encountering the fury in his gaze.

'As there seems to be nothing else for me to do here, with Rachel so expertly in charge, then if I want a job, I shall take one, Alex — whether you like it or not,' she announced bitterly, and turned on her heel to stalk back into the cottage, slamming the door behind her with a defiant crash.

# 5

Emma walked down to the village with a purposeful stride, still sparking with anger at Alex's domineering attitude.

What right did he have to tell her how she should spend her time? He was the one determined to keep Rachel, after all. Without her there, she would have plenty to do coping with the house and Jamie, but until Alex saw reason and that woman went, then, Emma decided, there was no reason why she shouldn't have a job of her own.

Brian Pendower greeted her with an enthusiastic smile of welcome from behind the bar.

'What a delightful pleasure. Does this mean you've come to look me over?'

'If you still want me,' she replied.

'Oh, I want you right enough,' he chuckled, putting an encircling arm round her shoulders. 'How about a tour of the premises first though.'

He guided her to the steep stairs, following a few steps behind and Emma, conscious of his gaze, slowed her pace a little, wishing she hadn't worn such a short skirt.

'Six guest rooms,' Brian stated, opening one. 'Each with adjoining bathroom.'

She edged past him as he held the door, feeling his body press slightly against hers as she did so, and studied the luxurious fittings in the room. Pale ivory silk covers and curtains, similar in style to those of her own bedroom in the cottage, probably from the same interior designer, she decided.

'Only three rooms are occupied at the moment, but it will get busier from June onwards.'

'Then the bookings won't take up much time,' she pointed out, easing her way out again carefully as he leaned nonchalantly against the door.

'No,' he agreed, 'but we do a large number of meals during the summer months, both at lunchtime and in the evenings, and those require careful coordination to prevent any delay or overbooking. Then there's the occasional special function; wedding receptions, birthday or anniversary parties, club evenings and that sort of thing. It's surprising how popular we are here.'

'What kind of hours were you thinking of?'

'Whatever suits you, my dear. A pretty face to welcome folk doesn't go amiss, so the longer you're here the better for all concerned. I'm sure we can come to some amicable arrangement.'

'I need to be home when Jamie comes out of school, so perhaps if I was here in the mornings, until about three o'clock or so, then I could collect him on my way back there?' she suggested. 'I'm afraid Alex isn't at all keen on the idea though,' she added ruefully.

'No,' Brian replied slowly. 'I doubt he would be. Would you like a coffee? Or maybe stay for a bite of lunch? It would give you some idea of how busy we are.'

'Don't you and Alex get on very well?' Emma questioned, observing the swift way he changed the subject.

Brian gave an abrupt laugh. 'Not exactly, but how astute of you to notice, my dear. I thought we concealed it rather well.'

'So why?' she persisted. 'Surely, living here, you have a great deal in common.'

'The only thing we ever had in common was Louise.'

Emma stared back at him, eyes wide.

'You mean you were once her boyfriend?'

He laughed again.

'Boyfriend? What a delightful expression. Yes, you could say that, I suppose. Now, how about that coffee. We'll take it out into the sunshine, shall we?'

His hand rested lightly on her waist as he guided her outside to a small patio where white ironwork chairs and tables overlooked the sea.

Emma sat down, shading her eyes until he'd put up the striped umbrella above the table, wondering whether she was imagining the pressure of his thigh against hers as she stirred sugar into the pretty flowered cup.

'How about starting tomorrow?' he announced and she nodded vaguely, trying to gauge just how old he was.

The neatly trimmed hair was thick and a distinguished grey, while the deep tan on his skin showed deeply etched lines that could have been caused by too much sun. His neck, always the give-away, was partly hidden by a mustard-yellow silk cravat tucked into a scarlet striped shirt, worn under a well-cut navy blazer.

She studied the outline of his chin, noticing the slight thickening around his jaw. He must be in his fifties at least, she decided.

'Tomorrow then,' she said, finishing the coffee and rising to her feet.

'Won't you stop and have lunch with me?' he pleaded, leaning closer, and she saw for the first time that the pale blue iris of his eyes was yellow-rimmed and bloodshot. 'I haven't explained the reception side of things yet.'

'Well, I . . . ' she began.

'No excuses, my dear. We should do everything correctly, shouldn't we?'

His hand was warm on her back as he took her indoors again, showing her the dining-room and kitchen, then the curved desk near the bar where she would be working.

'Where I can keep an eye on you,' he smiled.

The bar was already crowded, the local fishermen mingling with tourists who were passing through the village and had stopped to view the pretty little harbour, intrigued by the boats being unloaded of their catch.

'Shouldn't you be working?' Emma enquired later, when he took her to a corner table and handed her the menu.

'If you're the boss, you can do as you please and Williams is quite capable of managing the bar on his own for once in a while. Besides, I have to eat, you know — and I certainly don't want to miss the opportunity of having such fascinating and desirable company.'

He took the crimson napkin from the table and placed it over her lap, his fingers hesitating for a second on her thighs as he smoothed it flat, and she glanced quickly up at him, but saw only a bland and innocent expression on his face.

'The lasagne is good,' he advised.

'I really should get back. Rachel will wonder what's happened to me.'

'Do you honestly think she'll care?' he laughed.

'Well, no,' she admitted. 'I don't suppose she will.'

With a well practised hand he filled her glass, raising his in a toast.

'To our future together, Emma, my dear.'

* * *

There was a taut atmosphere between them that evening when Emma and Alex ate their meal. She felt full up from her delicious midday lunch and picked at the glutinous mess of macaroni cheese Rachel had made, while Alex was still fuming after her announcement that she was starting work at 'The Smugglers' the following morning.

As Rachel was eating with them, they could only glare at each other and wait until they reached the privacy of the lounge to continue the argument that had started earlier.

'You know my feelings about that man, Emma, and you're being totally unreasonable.'

'You're the one who's being totally unreasonable, Alex. I've already told you I'm not prepared to spend my days twiddling my thumbs and yet you're quite adamant about keeping Rachel on here. And besides . . . ' She paused, watching his reaction through half-lowered lashes, 'I find Brian rather charming.'

The effect of her words was like a match to dry tinder.

'Then all I can say, Emma,' Alex replied through tight lips, 'is that I hope you don't live to regret it — and neither do I.'

With that he strode from the room and seconds later she saw him cross the garden and disappear through the gate into the field, going towards the beach.

He's jealous, Emma decided with a surge of pleasure, and went out to join him, running eagerly through the long grass until she caught up with him near the cliff edge, throwing her arms round his neck as he turned, fired by the fierceness of his mouth as it closed over hers.

'I love you, Alex,' she whispered softly, linking her fingers in the thick thatch of his hair. 'There'll never be anyone else.'

Then, as he held her, his lips nuzzling her ear lobe, she heard his sudden gasp of shock and pulled away, following the line of his gaze.

Across the lawn near the cottage a woman was strolling, her long blonde hair swinging round the shoulders of her wide-necked peacock-blue dress.

'What's the matter, Alex?' Emma cried, frightened by the expression on his face.

'Louise,' he murmured faintly, his body rigid as he stood, the blood drained from his skin.

'Don't be silly,' she said. 'It's just someone visiting. Let's go back and see who it is.'

He stumbled over the uneven ground, his legs stiff and unbending, following her mechanically, but by the time they reached the cottage, the woman had disappeared.

'I expect Rachel's let her in,' Emma observed, pushing open the door of the kitchen where Rachel was tying on her apron, ready to wash the dishes. 'Is she in the lounge?'

The flint-grey eyes looked blankly back at her.

'Who?' Rachel asked.

'There was a lady in the garden,' Emma explained.

'No one's called.'

'But you must have seen her, Rachel. She was crossing the lawn, right outside this window. A blonde woman in a blue dress.'

Rachel turned her head sharply to stare questioningly at Alex.

'We both saw her, Rachel,' he told her in a shaken voice.

'No one's been here,' Rachel repeated.

'Perhaps she'd strayed off the path then and merely took a short cut out through the gate,' Emma suggested, worried by Alex's expression.

'Probably,' he replied flatly, his eyes still searching the garden with a tortured expression.

'Can we go into Falmouth on Saturday?' she asked, changing the subject adroitly, pulling him gently into the lounge where the evening sun streamed in through the diamond-shaped panes.

'Falmouth?' he questioned distractedly. 'What for?'

'New furniture,' Emma told him.

'What's wrong with all this?' he asked, glancing round the room.

'Not this,' she said. 'Our bedroom, and Jamie's. His is such a jumble of old junk. And as for ours — I hate those twin beds.'

A faint smile eased the worry from his eyes.

'Do you? So do I. They're a bit inhibiting, aren't they?'

'And all those dreadful mirrors . . . '

'Louise chose those.'

'Then it's time for a change, Alex,' she replied firmly.

'Falmouth it is then, darling,' he said, kissing her, but she could still detect a hint of anguish in his look.

★  ★  ★

Jamie was full of excitement when she told him.

'Won't I have to have that horrid old wardrobe any more?'

'No, it's so gloomy.'

117

'Things could live in there, you know,' he suggested, eyeing her sideways.

'Woodworm, you mean?'

He shook his head.

'Not woodworms, silly. Things. Goblins and witches and ghosts.'

'Oh Jamie!' Emma laughed, giving him a hug. 'There aren't such things.'

He gave her a wary look.

'There might be,' he said. 'And they could live in my wardrobe.'

'Has that been worrying you, Jamie?'

He nodded reluctantly, lowering his eyes from hers.

'Then the sooner it goes, the better,' she replied, dropping a kiss on the top of his fair head.

'Is Rachel going to have new furniture too?'

Emma hesitated.

'If she wants to, I suppose.'

'Shall I ask her?'

'If you like.'

Jamie wriggled from her lap and rushed off to the kitchen, returning minutes later looking rather subdued.

'She said it's a wicked waste of money and no thank you very much.'

'Good. Then it'll be just the three of us going,' Emma smiled.

She was at the reception desk and wearing a neat black gaberdine suit and crisp white cotton blouse when Brian came through into the bar the following day.

'Emma! You look most efficient. What a splendid impression you're going to create, my dear,' he beamed. 'And black stockings, I see,' he added, glancing down at the shapely lines of her legs. 'Very alluring.'

'It doesn't look too severe, does it?' she asked anxiously. 'I wore this kind of outfit in London, but it might be rather out of place down here.'

'You look positively ravishing. I shan't be able to keep my eyes off you all day.'

Emma didn't find the work taxing. Her main task seemed to be allocating tables for lunch and dinner and trying to estimate a suitable time gap between each, so that the diners wouldn't overlap and be kept waiting.

'But how can I tell how long they'll take to eat?' she wailed to Brian. 'I'll never be able to judge that and those waiting will be furious.'

'After a few drinks at the bar, and a smile from my beautiful receptionist, I doubt anyone's going to complain, my dear,' he comforted, patting her cheek.

Within a couple of days she found herself getting to know more of the local residents who came in, greeting them by name and chatting, which made her life more interesting.

'So this is where you are,' Mrs Trellissick remarked, appearing one lunchtime to book a table for Sunday lunch. 'Jamie told us at news-time that Emma went to the pub every day and it caused me great alarm. I must say I'm very relieved to discover that it's only a job.'

'How's Jamie getting on?' Emma enquired.

'Much more talkative. Our news-time is getting quite enthralling. I'm afraid we're hearing an awful lot about what goes on in your household, Mrs Crawley. Still it does make a change from 'My dad caught three cod today' or 'My gran's got the twinges back in her knees again',' she laughed.

★  ★  ★

On Saturday, just as Emma and Jamie were climbing into the car with Alex, Rachel appeared.

'May I have a lift as well?' she asked, clutching a large zip-up bag. 'As you're going into Falmouth, I'd like to do some shopping. I'll make my own way home, of course.'

'Certainly, Rachel. Would you like to come in the front, then Emma can sit with Jamie.'

'He may well be travel sick,' Rachel informed her, turning round.

'I know. You've mentioned it before — several times,' said Emma. 'That's why we have a plastic bowl.'

He wasn't though and chattered away to Emma, pointing out everything he could see as they passed, and singing the latest pop songs with her, much to Rachel's disapproval.

'Are you quite sure you don't want a lift back, Rachel?' Alex enquired politely when they reached the car park in the square.

'No thank you. I'll probably visit my sister near Helston this afternoon. I'll come back from there.'

'Goodbye then. Have a pleasant day,' Emma said quickly, seeing her hesitate, determined that Rachel wasn't going to accompany them in their hunt for suitable furniture.

The tour of the local shops proved to be rewarding and by lunchtime they'd selected a complete bedroom suite with king-size bed for their room and a fitted unit of a bed with matching white-painted wardrobe and chest of drawers combined for Jamie.

'Can we have lunch in a burger bar?

Everyone in my class at school does and I've never ever had one,' he pleaded.

'If we must,' Alex sighed and met Emma's laughing eyes as she whispered, 'Old fogey,' in his ear.

They chose a window table and sat there munching the thick buns and onion-flavoured burgers, watching the crowds jostle past on the pavement, when suddenly Jamie let out a shriek and jumped off his chair to run to the door.

'Look, there's mummy.'

On the other side of the road a woman was hurrying through the crush of people. A woman with long blonde hair and wearing a low-necked peacock-blue dress.

Emma saw Alex's whitening fingers clench at the edge of the table as he stared across at her, then raced to catch Jamie before he disappeared into the street.

This can't be happening, Emma told herself. Louise is dead.

Through the steamed-up window she

could see Jamie and Alex on the other side of the road now, standing, their eyes searching, while people pushed past them, but the woman had vanished.

Emma sat, waiting, until they came back to the table, Jamie's small face bewildered and bleak.

'It wasn't mummy, darling,' she said gently, smoothing back his hair and looking deep into his tear-filled eyes. 'She isn't here any more. You know that, don't you?'

He stared back at her for a long thoughtful second, then nodded silently.

Emma wished she could comfort Alex as easily.

He sat, slumped over the table, his chin resting on his clenched hands, gazing out at the crowded street, his blue eyes anguished.

'Shall we go home now?' Emma suggested.

'But what about the boat?' Jamie demanded, jerking up his head. 'You promised we could go on a boat, daddy.'

Emma looked questioningly at Alex.

'I did,' he said ruefully. 'Over to St. Mawes.'

'Please, daddy.'

It's amazing, Emma thought, just how quickly a child's thoughts can be diverted. His mother's completely forgotten now.

'I did promise,' Alex said, 'and in the circumstances, maybe it'll take his mind off what's happened, but if you feel you'd rather . . . '

'Of course not,' she put in quickly.

It would be a relief to do something different — and perhaps they'd both forget.

They walked along to the small jetty further back in the town and down steep stone steps onto the ferry boat waiting there. Jamie knelt on the wooden seat to peer over the side into the murky water.

'Careful!' Emma warned, worried in case he leaned too far.

'Can we go to see the castle, daddy? Is it like the one we've got? Mrs Trissick told us all about them. They're on opposite sides so's the soldiers can guard the harbour from enemies. Are there still enemies?'

An anxious look spread over his face.

'How will the soldiers know we're not enemies and shoot us with cannon balls?'

'They don't do that any more, Jamie. That only happened when there was a war,' Alex explained.

With a spurt of sound and heavy smell of burning fumes the little boat shook into life. Jamie clutched the seat tightly, the fine hair lifting from his forehead as the ferry moved away from the shelter of the jetty and out towards the sea.

'Is it very deep?' he questioned, staring at the green water.

'Very,' said Alex.

'What happens if this boat sinks? Will we all drown?'

'No,' answered his father. 'See under there? Those are life rafts and we'd all hold on to them until another boat came and rescued us.'

Emma could see the relief that filled the little boy's eyes and smiled.

'Look,' she said, staring up at the grey stone building. 'There's Pendennis castle, all square and angular. See, on the hill up there? And that's St. Mawes castle across the water, all rounded and shaped like a clover-leaf.'

'And that's a windsurfer,' Jamie told her, obviously bored, pointing at the red and white striped sail skimming towards them. 'Are we going to run it over? How does that man make it go where he wants it to go?'

While Alex was explaining all the intricacies of windsurfing, Emma leaned back against the wooden seat, feeling the warmth of the sun on her skin, enjoying the freshness of the salt air as they moved over the water, watching them together. Jamie's face was intent, listening to every word his father spoke, nodding every now and then or questioning things he couldn't understand.

Alex is so patient with him, she thought, carefully pointing out and explaining everything — the huge ships, the skimming yachts, the bobbing buoys and what the white lighthouse at the foot of the cliffs was there for, as they passed it on the crossing.

Every so often one or other would smile across at her, as if to tell her she was included, even though they weren't actually talking to her.

We're growing to be a proper family now, she thought contentedly.

The seaweed-draped walls of the harbour at St. Mawes was rapidly coming into view now; to its right green, round-topped hills where a row of single pines stood out stark against the clear skyline, and then the town with its tiny shops and pretty cottages climbing up the steep incline towards the castle, almost hiding the pointed spire of the grey-roofed church.

Yachts drifted against the shoreline, leaning sideways to catch the wind and seagulls hung low in a frantic gathering over the water, screeching and diving, as they followed a loaded fishing-boat back to the crane — edged dock at Falmouth.

With a slight bump the ferry touched the wall and a jean-clad boy jumped across to tie its heavy ropes, drawing the boat closer.

'Are we going to see the castle now?' Jamie clamoured impatiently.

'It's quite a walk,' Alex warned. 'Maybe we'd better have an ice-cream first.'

'After those burgers?' Emma gasped, and wished she hadn't mentioned them when Alex's eyes clouded slightly and she knew he was remembering the woman.

'Can I have one with a chocolate thing in it?' Jamie asked.

'Please,' Emma reminded.

'Please can I have one with a chocolate thing in it?' he said obediently.

Alex's arm was round her shoulders as they began the climb, stopping to admire the tiny secluded gardens tucked behind stone walls and almost hanging over the edge of the cliff, separated by the road from the cottages opposite.

'It's a long way,' Jamie sighed, trying to stop the gathering stream of melted ice-cream that was running down his cornet with a frantic tongue, his mouth already coated with a generous layer of chocolate.

'Nearly there,' Emma comforted, catching his sticky hand to help him up the last steep bend.

'Did the soldiers really shoot people with all those guns?' he asked, when at last they were inside the thick walls, his face upraised to hers in eagerness. 'And look at those spikes!' he marvelled.

They toured the cold dank rooms, with Jamie darting from side to side to peer through slit-like windows or stare wonderingly up the dark chimneys of fireplaces, giving them an excited running commentary of everything he saw.

Outside again in the bright sunshine, they wandered down the sloping gardens to the edge of the water, looking out to watch enormous ships moving steadily along the Carrick Roads, while the flamboyant sails of yachts wove their dashing way round them.

'It amazes me how all these plants grow so well here,' Alex commented, his gaze fixed on the pale pink heads of hydrangeas just coming into bloom. 'They must catch the full force of every gale and yet my father has terrible trouble with his further inland.'

'Is it teatime yet?' Jamie asked plaintively, jumping down from one of the low stone walls into his father's arms.

'Where do you put it all?' Alex laughed, swinging him round and round. 'You're as light as a bag of feathers.'

'In here,' his son replied, pulling up his T-shirt and patting his small round tummy proudly. 'One day I'll be as big as you and grandpa.'

Right down by the harbour-side they found a restaurant, its low-beamed room stretching far back with dark wood tables and benches against the walls, where they sat and ate huge crisp toasted tea-cakes dripping with butter and drank strong tea from an enormous pot that seemed to go on for ever.

On the ferry back to Falmouth Emma pulled her windcheater more closely round her, feeling the sharpness of the wind as the sun began to sink in the sky. Jamie was leaning against Alex, his eyes heavy with sleep, his face relaxed and blissful. And Alex — her gaze turned to him, and her heartbeat quickened as she met the look he gave her, a look of deep contentment.

If only life could always be like this, she wished fervently. If only there was no Louise, or Rachel.

# 6

Emma could see that Alex was growing more troubled. He tried hard not to show it, but there was a permanent expression of anxiety in his eyes and she noticed he kept looking sideways and behind him wherever they went.

But what disturbed her even more was the yawning gulf that seemed to be stretching between them — as if Alex was reluctant to touch or make love to her. Could it be that he was already growing tired of her? Or was it that he still loved the image of his first wife and seeing that woman had made him realise it once and for all?

'Tell me more about Louise,' Emma requested of Brian a few days later.

'More? What exactly do you want to know?'

'Well, everyone keeps telling me how beautiful she was; describe her to me.'

'I can do better than that,' he said with a smile. 'Give me five minutes.'

She watched his straight back in its immaculate navy blazer move away from the bar and out into the corridor, then minutes later he returned, carrying a red leather album.

'This is Louise,' he said triumphantly, opening it to reveal pages of glossy coloured photographs.

Taking it from him, Emma found she was suddenly reluctant to discover what she most wanted to know, forcing herself to gaze down at the book waiting in front of her, dreading to open it.

The first page was filled with close-ups of a lovely face framed by thick pale gold hair that hung smoothly to tanned bare shoulders. Finely arched brows curved over eyes that were almost violet with wide high cheek bones beneath them; the nose was straight and narrow; the mouth full and petulant, pouting slightly.

With nervous fingers, Emma turned

the page. Louise smiled provocatively back at her, dressed in a tiny peacock-blue bikini that revealed far more than it concealed of smooth golden skin. Her figure was perfect, full-breasted and narrow-hipped.

On the next page Louise wore a sea-blue sundress, low-necked, tied with narrow strings, that emphasised her slender waist and billowed out in a gust of wind to reveal her long shapely legs against a background of dark granite grey cliffs.

The fourth page was of Louise, this time in winter or autumn, wearing a thick angora jumper and tightly fitting trousers in the same shade of blue. She was posed on a fallen tree trunk, sitting sideways, her figure silhouetted in its full rounded beauty.

Emma continued to the end of the book, growing more despondent with every page. No wonder Alex loved her. She was every man's fantasy woman.

'Bewitching, wasn't she?' Brian murmured, leaning over her shoulder.

'Did she always wear that colour? Peacock-blue,' asked Emma curiously.

'Always. It suits her, doesn't it? She knew that and made it a sort of gimmick, never wearing anything else.'

'I rather wish you hadn't shown me,' Emma said mournfully. 'Now I know what I'm up against.'

'Don't be silly,' Brian laughed, his fingers lightly brushing her cheek. 'You're an extremely attractive girl yourself.'

'Not like that.'

'No,' he agreed. 'Not like that, but then I doubt Alex would want you to be.'

'What do you mean?'

'I've told you before that every man who saw Louise wanted her.'

His pale eyes were watching her closely as he continued.

'And most of them succeeded.'

For a moment she gazed back at him with puzzled eyes.

'You mean, she had *lovers*?'

Brian nodded. 'Don't sound so

shocked. Women frequently do, you know.'

'Even after she was married to Alex?' questioned Emma in a disbelieving tone.

He nodded again.

'But how *could* she?'

His mouth curled into a sardonic smile. 'Very easily, I can assure you.'

'Poor Alex,' she said.

'Poor Alex indeed,' he agreed.

'What did he do about it?'

'There wasn't much he could do. A woman like Louise would never be content with one man in her life. Alex soon realised that.'

'And yet he still loved her?'

'I often wonder,' Brian replied thoughtfully. 'And now he's chosen you.'

His fingers lingered on hers as he bent to take the photograph album and his voice lowered. 'Are you like Louise, Emma?'

Emma pulled her hand away indignantly.

'Of course not!'

'They do say a man always marries the same type of woman. It happens time after time.'

'Well, I can assure you Alex hasn't.'

At that moment, the telephone rang and Emma turned to answer it thankfully. The conversation was getting far too convoluted and she was becoming increasingly uneasy about Brian's manner.

Alex's words echoed in her head. 'The morals of a tom-cat'. She'd watched him with other women at the bar, seeing their reaction to him. He was very attractive, she had to admit. He quite obviously enjoyed a woman's company, but she was growing to dislike the fact that he always had to touch in some way, a bare arm, a shoulder, a knee, his fingers caressing the skin, his body accidently brushing as he passed.

Had he, too, been one of Louise's lovers? And was that why Alex hated him so much?

It was June now, the days stretched to their longest, evenings still warm when Alex returned home. They took to swimming in the sea or walking along the firm, tide-wet sand, skirting the rocks that jutted out here and there.

Yet all the time Alex was tense, his face haunted, growing thinner and more gaunt. Even when they were together, he couldn't relax.

'You're working too hard,' Emma told him, hating his remoteness, as they sat on a rock watching the waves curl in over the sand, leaving a line of glistening dark seaweed as they retreated again.

He shook his head.

'What's worrying you then, Alex? Please tell me,' she begged.

'Suppose Louise isn't dead?' he blurted out, turning agonised blue eyes to hers.

The shock of his words hit her, making her body go weak.

'Not dead? What do you mean? She was drowned, wasn't she?'

'There was a body,' he said slowly.

'But surely it was identified as Louise?'

'She'd been in the water a long time, Emma. It wasn't exactly easy.'

'Oh, Alex,' she whispered, burying her head against his shoulder. 'And now you think it might not have been Louise? That this woman we keep seeing . . .'

Her voice died away as the realisation of what she was saying hit her. 'But it can't be.'

'Mistakes do happen,' he said brokenly.

Her mind was racing. If Louise wasn't dead, then that meant . . . the thought was too horrible for her to even consider, but it came creeping back persistently like the waves on the beach.

That meant she and Alex weren't legally married. Louise could return and take up her life with him again. And Jamie . . .

She stared at Alex, trying to read the expression in his blue eyes and the one question that had haunted her for so long burned in her brain.

Did he still love Louise?

It was something she couldn't bring herself to ask him, dreading the truth.

Instead she reached out a tentative hand to touch his cheek and found it caught in a fierce grip as he lifted it to his lips and kissed it fervently.

'What have I done to you?' he whispered. 'I swept you off your feet and carried you away before you had even a chance to think properly — because I wanted you so much and was terrified of losing you. I've been so unfair. If I'd told you the truth — about Louise, about Jamie — you'd never have married me.'

'Oh, but I would,' she declared hotly. 'It wouldn't have made any difference at all.'

'If I'd told you all the truth, it would,' he said quietly.

A flicker of fear ran through her.

'What else is there to tell me?' she breathed, the frantic beat of her heart threatening to choke her.

'That I murdered my wife.'

The surge of the waves roared in her ears, pounding with the fierce beat of her heart. Her vision blurred, seeing the green depths grow hazy and fade. She tried to breathe, her chest bound suddenly in the grip of iron bands.

Alex looked down at her, his fingers tenderly tracing the outline of her face.

'I left Louise to drown, Emma.'

'Tell me . . . what happened.'

Her voice was only a faint whisper.

'Louise was beautiful. I was drawn to her because of that. But there was nothing else to her. She was shallow. A lovely face. A magnificent body. Nothing more. No depths. No feelings. Only caring for herself. I realise that now, knowing you as I do. You're so very different.'

He was clasping her hand as if he could never let it go.

'It was months before it dawned on me that there was someone else. I don't know how I could have been so dense, so unobservant, when it was happening there, right in front of me. Louise and Brian. When I questioned her about it, she was quite open. She found him fascinating — as you do.'

Emma flinched, remembering how she'd taken a delight in teasing Alex about Brian, enjoying the thought that he was jealous.

'I discovered they were meeting, down on the beach, in the caves. She was devious at first, but then she grew careless. It must have been so easy for her.'

A tell-tale pulse was flickering in his jaw, revealing the emotions that were surging through him.

'Each day she would take Jamie with her for a walk. The child was only three.'

His mouth tightened into a narrow line.

'One afternoon — a Friday — I came home early. It was a bank holiday weekend. Everyone went home soon after lunch that day. Jamie and Louise had gone down to the beach, Rachel told me. I went across the garden, through the field to the cliffs. It was beautiful. Hot sunshine. The promise of a glorious weekend.'

Emma saw him swallow hard, before he continued.

'Jamie was sitting on the grass, all by himself, not far from the cliff-edge. I was horrified. I took his hand and he began to cry, refusing to move from the spot. 'Mummy says I mustn't,' he sobbed.'

Emma was alert now, remembering that place on the cliff path that Jamie would never pass, no matter how hard she tried to persuade him, obstinately standing there, not venturing further.

'I was furious, tugging him along, determined to find Louise and demand to know why she'd left him there alone like that. And then I heard her laugh. A low throbbing laugh. I'd heard it so many times before — and I knew its meaning.'

Alex turned his tormented gaze to Emma.

'They were in one of the caves. Louise and Brian. Jamie was standing there beside me. What could I do? I wanted to smash the man to pulp. Louise was my wife — and Brian was supposed to be my friend.

'They heard Jamie whimper, and eventually Louise came out, wearing a skimpy little bikini. A pretty blue. She always wore blue. Then she saw me. I think for once in her life she was terrified. And Brian followed. He had that smug, satisfied look on his face that I hate so much. He didn't even seem to care.

'I can't remember what I said to them. All I know is I was almost out of my mind with anger — and Jamie was crying, sobbing his heart out, frightened by the fury of what was happening.

'Brian only made one comment. It was enough, though, for me to hit him right across the mouth and I saw his nose begin to spurt blood with the force of it. Then he made off across the beach, back to the inn, like a scared whippet.

'Louise stood there, taunting me, telling me what a fantastic lover Brian was, what he did, how she felt . . . I couldn't stand it any longer.'

Emma sat, her eyes wide with fear, waiting for him to continue, waiting to know, not daring to breathe.

'Finally she turned and plunged into the sea, thinking I'd go after her, pleading with her as I always did when we argued, wanting to make things right again. I was so very weak where she was concerned; and she knew it.

'She looked fantastically beautiful. Her body golden as she stood, the waves crashing round her, soaking into her hair, glistening on her skin. And yet, at that moment, I knew how much I hated her.

'Jamie was still crying, terrified of the malevolence blazing round him. I bent down and picked him up, his tiny body shaking with sobs. Louise was a long way out by now, her arms cutting through the water, swimming strongly. There was a fast current running and the tide was on the turn. I knew that, but I didn't care. It would serve her right, I thought.

'Looking down from the top of the track I could see her, barely visible, still swimming away from the shore.'

He breathed in deeply, closing his eyes for a second.

'It was weeks before her body was found. Weeks in the sea, battered by the rocks, and the fish . . . I had to identify her.'

A shudder ran through his taut body.

'I recognised the bright blue of her bikini strings, still tied round her waist. That was all . . . '

Emma took him in her arms, holding him close, feeling herself tremble from the force of the emotion that tore through his body. Then he raised his head, his eyes still wet with tears, and said quietly,

'And so you see I murdered her, Emma, just as if I'd held her down and watched her drown.'

'Of course you didn't, Alex,' she protested. 'Louise chose to swim out to sea. She knew the risks. She swam there often. It was her own fault. Not yours.'

He gazed back at her sadly. 'I only wish you were right.'

'But I am,' she insisted. 'There was nothing you could do. Jamie needed you far more than Louise at that moment. And if you had gone after her, would she have come back? From what you say she'd have fought against you. There was nothing you could do, Alex.'

Gently his lips brushed hers.

'I love you, Emma. I love you so very much.'

'What are we going to do? How can we find out who this woman is?' she asked. 'We've got to know.'

'Suppose it is Louise?'

'How can it be?'

'It could easily have been another woman in the sea,' he said.

'Wearing Louise's bikini?' scorned Emma.

'I could have been wrong. There was very little left of it. All I know is it was blue, the colour Louise always wore.'

'The coincidence is too great, Alex. Two women of similar build, fair-haired, wearing the same kind of bikini. It's far too unlikely.'

'But it happens,' he insisted.

'It happens,' she had to admit in defeat, 'but now explain to me why Louise has waited three years before turning up again?'

'Maybe she went off with another man,' he suggested.

'You said Brian was her lover.'

'There were others,' he replied dully.

'Okay, suppose it *is* Louise. You can divorce her. She's been gone for over three years, leaving you and her child. That's grounds for divorce,' reasoned Emma, then paused, before continuing reluctantly. 'Or maybe you don't want to do that. Maybe you still love her.'

She had to know the truth.

'I told you,' he said impatiently. 'I hated her.'

'At that moment you did. There on the beach — with Brian — but do you still feel so strongly?'

Just the sight of a woman dressed in the same coloured clothes affected him, she knew, or was it just the feeling of guilt he still retained, blaming himself for her terrible death?

'How can I convince you that there is only one woman in my life and that woman is you?' he implored brokenly.

'I don't know, Alex. I don't know what to think any more.'

She knew as soon as she'd said the words that she was only adding to his torture, seeing the expression that tightened his face, and full of remorse caught at his hand, burying her head against his shoulder.

'I'm sorry, Alex. It's just that my whole world seems to be crumbling round me. I don't know how to cope.'

He kissed her hair, her forehead, her tear-wet eyes, her quivering lips, his fingers softly caressing the nape of her neck.

'And it's all my fault, Emma darling. I should never have married you.'

She raised her face to his.

'You didn't know Louise would come back,' she said. 'If it is Louise.'

'Who else could it be?' he asked in a resigned voice.

'Coincidence, like I keep saying. People often have a double. We've only seen her from a distance, haven't we? Up close she probably doesn't resemble her at all.'

'But what about Jamie? He thinks it's his mother.'

She'd forgotten Jamie.

'But why?' she asked. 'He was only three when Louise was drowned. Why should he even remember what she looked like?'

'Well, it seems he does,' Alex replied flatly.

'We're probably getting hysterical over nothing, you know,' she comforted. 'A blonde wearing peacock-blue. That's all it is.'

But when she saw the look in Alex's

eyes, she knew he wasn't convinced.

'Let's go somewhere different this weekend. Get away from here, just for a while,' she suggested.

'We could,' he said doubtfully.

'You know the area. Where shall it be?'

'How about Cotehele? It's a beautiful house. National Trust. One of my favourites. Set in woods leading down to the Tamar, over near Saltash. We could spend the day there. Jamie's due for a visit to my parents. We can drop him off on the way.'

'Oh, Alex! Is that fair?'

'He'll have the time of his life. They spoil him dreadfully. And he'd probably be bored stiff visiting a stately home.'

★  ★  ★

Rachel heard the news with a frown.

'Mr and Mrs Crawley always feed the child with the most unsuitable things,' she grumbled. 'Last time he informed me he'd eaten three fried sausages with

152

chips. Your parents seem to live on that kind of food and you know how bad it is for anyone. I always avoid giving him anything steeped in fat.'

'Come on now, Rachel! You know my mother grills everything,' chided Alex. 'The odd occasion won't hurt him and anyway, it doesn't seem to have harmed my parents, does it? They're well into their seventies now.'

She gave a slight sniff.

'And probably have hearts layered in fat too,' she replied acidly.

'Somehow I doubt it, judging by the way they attack a croquet ball,' Alex smiled.

Jamie was delighted. 'Grandma has a great big tin full of sweets,' he confided to Emma. 'And she always lets me have a handful to bring home.' He gave a wicked little chuckle. 'I let Grandpa take them out for me though. His hands are much bigger.'

'You're a naughty little imp,' she laughed, sitting on her heels to give him a hug, delighted when he snuggled close and hugged her too.

And then, over the top of his fair head, she caught sight of the look on Rachel's face, staring down at them, and a slight shiver ran down her spine.

★ ★ ★

'This'll be the first time you've met my parents, Emma,' Alex said as they settled themselves into the car, ready for the journey.

She nodded, feeling a little apprehensive.

'There's no need to worry, darling,' he smiled. 'They're not ogres. Tell Emma what grandma and grandpa are like, Jamie.'

'Very old people, with crinkly faces that smile all the time,' he reported solemnly. 'Grandpa has a stick when he walks about 'cos his leg's gone wobbly and he's got quite a shiny head where his hair's worn away. Will your hair do that one day, daddy?'

'Probably,' Alex replied ruefully,

running a hand through his thick thatch and glancing into the driving mirror as he did so.

'What about grandma?' Emma asked.

Jamie stared at her with surprised blue eyes. 'She's got lots of hair,' he told her. 'It's like cotton wool, all white and fluffy. She wears a floaty sort of scarf over it when we go out. It's a blue one — like her eyes. Grandma's got ever such blue eyes. A bit like daddy's,' he added, looking up into the driving mirror to see his father's reflection.

He knelt up on the back seat, squashing his nose against the window.

'We're nearly there, aren't we, daddy? It's down a windy, windy lane like a tunnel, with all the trees growing over the top,' he explained to Emma. 'They've got strawberries in their garden, haven't they, daddy? I picked them for our pudding last time and we had real thick cream too.'

'Was that after those sausages?' asked Emma mischievously.

Jamie shot her a conspiratorial

glance, obviously remembering Rachel's words too.

'Yes, but I wasn't sick. Rachel said I would be and I had to go to bed in my oldest pyjamas with a bit of towel over my pillow.'

The car was turning in white-painted gateposts now, the wheels crunching along a long gravel drive to stop outside a faded white-walled bungalow, half-hidden by the tall spikes of foxgloves bordering it. Somewhere behind it a motor-mower echoed.

With stiff limbs a grey-muzzled golden retriever rose heavily from the top step where it had been basking in the sunshine, its feathery tail waving slowly to and fro in greeting as it gave a rather hoarse bark.

The door was already open and a tiny bird-like woman came down the steps, her face beaming with pleasure.

'Where's my Jamie then?' she smiled, gathering the little boy into her arms as he jumped down from the car. 'Tom! They're here!' she called loudly, then turned back to them, shaking her head.

'It's no good. We'll have to go round there and find him. He's getting as deaf as a post. Now, let me have a good look at you, Emma, my dear. You're someone very special, from what my son tells me on the phone.'

Emma could see instantly what Jamie had meant about his grandma's eyes as their shrewd blueness gazed back at her and then a thin arm slipped through hers and gave it a little squeeze.

'I hope he's made a better choice than last time,' came the rather dry comment.

# 7

The tall straight figure striding behind the motor-mower was so like Alex that it gave Emma quite a shock. This is what my husband will be like in another thirty years or so, she thought, studying his father carefully.

'Tom!'

At the end of the lawn, the mower swung round for its return run, and he looked up with a start, bending quickly to switch it off.

Jamie was already racing across the grass to hurl himself into his grandpa's waiting arms and be swung round, legs flying behind him, shrieking with excitement.

'Emma, my dear.'

Her hand was grasped by a rough-ened muddy palm and shaken vigorously, warm eyes smiling down at her.

Even his smile's the same, she

thought, with a quick intake of breath.

'You do have time for coffee, don't you, Alex?' his mother questioned anxiously.

'You'd better,' laughed his father. 'She's been making scones and heaven knows what since crack of dawn.'

'Really, Tom!' his wife scolded.

'Of course we have, mother. It's only ten o'clock, but before you get carried away with your usual enthusiasm and fill us full to bursting, we're eating lunch at Cotehele and I've already told Emma what a treat she's in store for, so don't you dare blunt her appetite.'

'Come and help me then, Emma, will you? Then we can get to know each other properly.'

'And me,' Jamie reminded her. 'I always help you, don't I, grandma?'

'And you, scallywag,' she laughed, ruffling the fair hair. 'Well, what do you think of your new mummy then?'

'She's not my mummy,' he replied, glancing up with puzzled eyes. 'She's

Emma. You can't be a mummy until you have a baby.'

'Oh dear, I quite thought that's what he'd call you,' said his grandma, looking ruefully at Emma. 'Have I said the wrong thing?'

'Of course not,' she answered quickly, but even so a pang of sadness ran through her when she heard Jamie's words. One day, she'd hoped, he would regard her as his mother.

'Now then, my dear. Would you like to butter those scones for me, while I make the coffee? Jamie, there are some biscuits in the tin. Would you like to arrange them carefully on that plate? Wash your hands first. They look a bit muddy to me.'

The little boy stared down at them thoughtfully.

'I think that came off grandpa,' he said, dutifully turning on the tap when Emma lifted him up to the sink, and washed hers too.

'Carry them in to the other room now, will you, Jamie,' said his grandma, 'and tell daddy we'll be there in a minute.'

Once he was out of the kitchen, she turned to Emma with a smile and said, 'Now I've got you on your own, my dear, how are you getting on with that dreadful woman, Rachel? I quite thought Alex would have got rid of her by now, but then maybe you don't want to do that — he does tell me you're working, of course.'

'Only at 'The Smugglers' for a few hours during the morning and early afternoon. You see, there's nothing for me to do in the house with Rachel around and I do meet Jamie from school on my way home,' Emma hastened to inform her, sensing a slight disapproval.

'Louise chose her, you know. I really can't imagine why she couldn't cope with a baby. He was such a delightfully placid little chap. But then, it would've curtailed all her extra-marital activities, I suppose,' she commented drily.

'What did you think of her, Mrs

Crawley?' Emma asked. 'You must've known her pretty well over the years.'

Mrs Crawley turned bitter eyes on her.

'My daughter-in-law was a bitch, Emma. I can't describe her any other way, I'm afraid. I watched her torment my son the whole while she lived with him — and she enjoyed doing so. He worshipped her when they married. I've never seen a man more besotted: but Louise knew that and used it as a weapon.'

With a deft movement she placed delicately flowered china coffee cups on a silver tray and began to fill the sugar bowl.

'To be quite honest, it was the happiest day of my life when I heard she'd been drowned.'

Emma was surprised by the vehemence in Mrs Crawley's voice, noticing the flush that crept up her neck as she spoke.

'The only good thing in Louise's favour so far as I'm concerned is that she produced a delightful grandson for us. Apart from that, I disliked her intensely.'

'But she was beautiful?'

'In an extremely provocative sort of way, I suppose. Men found her very attractive. My husband did, I know. She appeared to make it her aim in life to lure any man into her web, old or young. That, of course, didn't endear her to me. He is Alex's father, after all. You'd have thought she'd have had some scruples.'

Emma placed the last scone on the dish and rewrapped the butter, putting it back in the larder, then opened the door for Mrs Crawley to go through.

When they'd finished their coffee, Alex and Emma left, with Jamie and his grandparents waving happily from the end of the drive.

'Don't rush back, will you,' smiled Mrs Crawley. 'It's not often we have the opportunity to spoil our grandson and we want to make the most of it.'

And as she wound the car window

up, Emma heard Jamie's voice asking eagerly, 'Is it those big, fat sausages for lunch, like we had last time, grandma?'

It was a gloriously sunny day and she leant back in her seat, watching the countryside roll past.

Alex drove smoothly, but fast, his hands light on the steering wheel, his eyes concentrating on the road ahead.

'Well, were they as bad as you feared?' he asked, turning his head slightly to catch her expression.

'They're delightful! I think your mother was a bit apprehensive herself though. She thought I might've been a second Louise.' Emma said the words deliberately, watching his reaction closely.

He gave a short laugh. 'I'm afraid mother never approved of Louise from the start and they were almost at daggers drawn as time went on. I used to visit them without her in the end. It led to a quieter life — and I didn't want Jamie upset while we were there.' The car swung round a corner and he changed gear, increasing power as they met the long straight road. 'He loves his grandparents so much and it seemed to annoy Louise, heaven knows why. It was as if she were jealous of the affection between them and yet she herself hardly took any notice of the child at all.'

'Maybe she resented anyone else sharing the love she wanted exclusively for her own,' Emma suggested.

'I don't think she loved Jamie in the slightest,' he said tersely. 'She totally ignored his existence.'

'That doesn't mean she didn't expect him to love her though. From what I'm learning about Louise it seems she needed to be the centre of attention and no one else should have what she claimed as hers alone.'

'Maybe,' he mused. 'Look, there's St. Austell.'

Emma turned her head to see the china clay tips rising like snow-capped mountains stark on the horizon to the right of them.

'There's an open-air museum there — Wheal Martyn. We must take Jamie some time. He'd love it.'

It was well past midday when they left Callington and turned down a steep narrow lane, then up through the tiny village of St. Dominick and down again to Cotehele.

Alex parked in the tree-bordered car park and guided her through a gate into the grounds.

'We'd better eat first,' he said, glancing at his watch. 'The restaurant's in that old barn over there.'

Together they went down the steps to find a table in the long, high-roofed room, its rough whitewashed walls hung with patterns of sickles and scythes and old smocks that had once been worn for working.

Despite her coffee and home-made scones earlier Emma already felt hungry and studied the menu eagerly, breathing in the savoury smell filling the air.

'What's the 'special' today?' Alex

166

asked the mob-capped girl who came to serve them.

'It's pork-in-cider hotpot, but I'll just check there's some left. Everyone's been keen to have it today.'

'That sounds rather filling,' Emma said, wrinkling up her nose as she continued to read the list. 'I must leave room for some of that delicious-looking chocolate gateau and clotted cream over there. It looks gorgeous.'

'Try one of the salads then,' Alex advised her, eyeing the meals other people were enjoying. 'The smoked mackerel looks rather good.'

When they'd finished eating and drained the last of the smooth dark coffee, they went through the cobbled courtyard and into the Hall of the grey-stone manor house, where the white walls were hung with an abundance of ancient swords, pistols, guns and armour.

An immense wooden table was almost lost in the centre of the rough stone floor, its polished surface laid with pewter plates, a beautiful bowl of deep-pink roses glowing near one end.

They moved on into the old dining-room where the walls, as in most of the rooms, were hung with enormous woven tapestries reaching almost to the floor and surrounding the wide, log-filled, open fireplace.

In the chapel Alex showed her the strange clock in an alcove.

'It's supposed to be the earliest in England and still working where it was first installed in the fifteenth century.'

'But it doesn't even look like a clock,' Emma protested, staring at the strange contraption of iron fixed to an oak beam, and listening to the deep rhythmic tick as it moved. 'It hasn't got a face.'

In the upper rooms she admired the extravagant four-poster beds, one with thickly embroidered Jacobean hangings, the huge flowers and leaves in pink and green; another with crimson drapery decorated with silk rosettes.

From the next bedroom Emma gazed

down through the narrow slits called peeps on one side into the Hall and on the other into the chapel.

'That was so the lord and lady of the manor could keep an eye on what was happening below,' Alex explained, seeing the look of enquiry on her face.

'I'd love a four-poster,' she sighed, staring longingly at the white quilted hangings embroidered with red wool.

'Why didn't you say so when we were choosing the new furniture in Falmouth then? We could easily have ordered one.'

'I didn't know then, did I?' she replied indignantly. 'I've never really seen one up close like this before and these are all so magnificent.'

'There are more to come,' Alex grinned, leading her up a flight of stone steps.

'Oh no,' Emma declared, shaking her head when she saw them. 'They're not as beautiful as those others.'

'You'll probably get beheaded for saying so then,' he laughed, consulting

169

the guide book. 'These are Queen Anne's and King Charles'.'

'Well, they're not so grand, nor are the rooms. This one's terribly dark and gloomy and the other's so small the bed almost fills it.'

She peered into a mirror on the wall.

'And I doubt King Charles could see much of himself in that either.'

'It's extremely rare, Emma. Made of steel in the sixteen-hundreds before ordinary looking-glasses came into fashion. He probably found it quite flattering too.'

'Well, he must have had an extremely distorted view of himself then.'

As they wandered along the winding paths meandering down through the garden to the river, Emma stopped to look inside a tiny chapel.

'This is rather a strange place to find one, isn't it?' she observed, looking round at the thick trees.

'Richard Edgcumbe who lived here in the late fourteen-hundreds had it built,' Alex told her, again consulting the guide book. 'Apparently he was being pursued by a baddie called Trenowth and his men and, having tucked a stone into his cap, threw it into the water, so that when they heard the splash and saw the floating cap, they thought he'd drowned himself and gave up the chase. Richard returned years later and built this chapel in thanks for being saved from capture and probable death.'

Ahead Emma could see a collection of old grey stone buildings clustered round the quay down by the river that glinted in the sunlight streaming through the trees, and hurried Alex on.

'There's a tea place over there,' she pointed. 'In that old pub.'

'You're surely not hungry again, darling? Not eating for two, are you?' he teased, glancing down at her slim waist and hips. 'You should've had the hotpot. It was extremely filling.'

'They do cream teas,' she hinted persuasively, ignoring his words. 'And anyway, it's almost a couple of hours since we had lunch.'

'We'll visit the little museum over there first,' he laughed. 'Then you can eat. I'd hate you to get too plump yet awhile.'

A pleasure boat filled with waving tourists went past, the voice of their guide echoing as it disappeared round a bend in the river.

'This used to be a busy place for trade years back, you know,' Alex told her. 'But the arrival of the railway at Calstock ruined all that. It was so much quicker to transport goods by rail instead of in sailing barges.'

He pulled her nearer the water.

'That's the old 'Shamrock',' he said, pointing to the long high-masted boat lying low in a shallow channel, 'a Tamar barge that's been restored in recent years. Isn't she beautiful?' But Emma had already disappeared through the low doorway of the museum in one of the old warehouse buildings and was following the progress of life as it had once been at Cotehele from the detailed drawings and notices on the walls.

'Did you know Queen Victoria actually came here?' she asked him, pleased to be able to impart some local knowledge herself.

'On August 21st 1846 in 'The Fairy' and wearing a green silk dress, lilac polka cloak and straw bonnet trimmed with heart's ease,' he replied smugly. 'I read it too!'

'Oh, come on, let's have that cream tea before they run out of them,' she laughed, catching at his hand and dragging him across the rough ground towards the Edgcumbe Arms, tucked away in a corner.

Another pleasure boat chugged its way between the steep banks, slowly passing the quay, leaving wide ripples across the water, and as Emma turned to watch it go by, her heart began to pound.

On the far side, half-hidden by the crowd of passengers, she caught a glimpse of sleek blonde hair, ruffled by the wind, and a bright peacock-blue dress.

Really, Emma thought shakily, I'm getting as paranoid as Alex. It's only a woman. There must be dozens around with blonde hair, and as for the dress, well it was a popular colour. She'd once had one herself, in a similar shade. It suited blondes.

Her eyes flickered up to Alex, thankful to see his head was turned to the entrance of the tea rooms. The boat would be gone in a second or two, safely hidden round the bend in the river. She glanced back to it, searching for the brilliance of the woman's dress. It was so unmistakeable, standing out clearly amongst all the other people.

Her heel stumbled on the rough ground and Alex instantly moved to catch her, his expression startled as her arms flew round his neck and she let herself slump against him, her face shielding his.

'Are you all right, Emma?' he questioned, his voice full of concern.

'Oh,' she gasped, pressing her forehead to his. 'I think I may have twisted my ankle slightly, but don't worry, I'll be fine when we get inside and I can sit down.'

Anxiously he guided her through the door and she quickly looked behind her to see the bow of the pleasure boat receding rapidly away from them, knowing that now he wouldn't see what she had seen.

'Is it swelling?' His fingers touched her ankle, probing gently.

Emma forced a slight wince of pain, sinking down onto a chair so that she faced the window and Alex took the one with his back to it.

At least she could see who was passing now and hopefully ward off any more unfortunate sightings. It seemed strange though, that wherever they went they seemed to see someone resembling Louise. Was it mere chance? Or deliberate?

'Not more cream gateau,' he grinned, watching her as she indicated her choice to the waitress. 'Do you practise all the seven deadly sins?'

Emma's gaze met his in puzzled surprise.

'Gluttony is one of them, my darling — and lust.'

'Surely that one's more in your line,' she countered sweetly. 'I wasn't the one to propose marriage so rapidly, don't forget.'

A shadow clouded his blue eyes, making her wish she hadn't uttered such a thoughtless remark.

'Do you regret it, Emma?' he asked slowly.

'Of course I don't,' she retorted, reaching out to clasp his hand. 'You know I don't.'

'Do I?' His eyes were doubtful. 'And will you always feel the same? Can you, with all this hanging over us?'

'Nothing's hanging over us, Alex,' she protested. 'Louise died three years ago. Can't you accept that?'

'Did she, Emma?'

'Of course she did.'

'That little performance outside didn't fool me, you know. I saw her too

— on the pleasure boat as it passed.'

With a sigh Emma stirred her tea. 'I'm sorry, Alex, but . . . '

'It was a good try, darling, but we've got to face up to the fact that Louise may not be dead and that any day now . . . '

'Then why doesn't she hurry up and do something?' Emma snapped. 'She really must have hated you, Alex, to torture you like this.'

'She has good reason,' he answered flatly. 'Don't forget I left her to die.'

'Oh, Alex, why do you keep saying that? Louise was a good swimmer. Everyone says so. The sea wasn't rough that day, was it? She could easily have swum back to the shore when ever she wanted.'

'There are currents out there, Emma. Treacherous ones that can sweep even the strongest swimmer away.'

'And Louise knew that. It was her own fault, not yours, Alex. She wanted to frighten you into going after her, but her plan went wrong. She was a bitch of a woman. Ask your mother.'

'My mother was jealous of her. Louise was a devastatingly attractive woman and . . . '

'Your father fancied her? Is that what you're going to say? From what I've heard Louise chased every man she saw, regardless of age. Your father wasn't an exception. Why won't you admit what she was really like, Alex? Why try to built up this saintly image of her in your mind? And you didn't kill her — Louise killed herself.'

'Then who . . . ?' There was ragged desperation in his anguished expression as he looked back at her.

'It's all in your imagination, Alex. You feel guilt for Louise's death. That's why every woman you see suddenly seems to look like her.'

'And what about Jamie? Is he suffering from a guilty conscience as well? How do you explain away his reaction? He saw her too, don't forget.'

Emma was stunned into silence. There was no way she could explain that and yet why should the child even remember what his mother had looked like? It was three years ago. Jamie was hardly more than a baby then. It just didn't make sense to her at all.

Grim-faced, Alex rose heavily to his feet. 'It's time we went back to collect him anyway. Rachel will be furious if we bring him home late for his bedtime.'

'Rachel!' The name exploded furiously from Emma's lips. 'You're Jamie's father, Alex. Don't you have any say in what your child does? You let Rachel rule the whole place and everyone in it. He's your son, not hers, Alex — and mine now too. If we want him to stay with his grandparents until well past his bedtime, that's our decision not bloody Rachel's.'

There was a shocked silence around them, tea cups held in stilled hands, heads swivelling, and Emma realised her voice had risen into a harridan's shriek.

Quickly she stood up, cheeks burning with humiliation, and walked outside into the sunshine, leaving Alex to pay and follow, his eyes like splinters of ice.

With rapid footsteps she headed towards the car park, head held erect, back taut, conscious of Alex rapidly catching up with her, then her arm was caught in the grip of fingers that bit into her bare skin.

'Don't you ever speak to me like that again,' he snarled, jerking her against his side.

'Why not? It's the truth, isn't it?' Her eyes were tear-filled as they glared up at him.

Abruptly he stopped in the middle of the path, staring bitterly back at her, while people pushed and jostled their way round them. Then his lips came down hard on her mouth, wrenching her head back as he held her tight against his lean, muscular body. For a second she resisted the force, holding herself taut and stiff, before giving in to the fierce heat of his kiss, her bones seeming to melt into his.

'I'm sorry, Emma,' he whispered, 'so very sorry.'

With forgiving fingers, she reached up to smooth the tense, angular planes of his face, leaning her forehead against the comfort of his shoulder.

'I'm sorry too . . . ' she murmured, her eyes searching his for the depth of love she knew was there, but they were gazing ahead, wide and startled as his arms dropped away from her and he moved suddenly forward. Emma turned, trying to see through the surrounding crush of people; then her heart plummeted like a stone, her breath caught in a rasp of pain at the sight of blonde hair stirring lightly over the shoulders of a bright blue dress dappled by the shadows of the trees. Alex was running, one word tearing from his lips. 'Louise!'

Emma felt the knife-edged sound shiver through her. Leadenly her legs propelled her forward, her body reluctant to follow.

Alex had reached the woman now,

his hand stretching out to catch her arm, swinging her round to face him.

Emma closed her eyes, not wanting to see any more.

# 8

Emma could hear Alex shouting through a confusion of shocked voices.

'Who are you, woman, and why, for heaven's sake, are you tormenting me like this?'

'Leave her alone, can't you?'

'Who do you think you are?'

'Bloody nutter!'

'Get the police, someone.'

Terrified, she pushed her way through the threatening group of people gathering round him. 'Alex!'

Someone turned to her. 'Is he with you?' She nodded, trying to force herself nearer. The blonde woman was standing, white-faced, staring with panic-stricken eyes at Alex.

'Please don't be frightened,' Emma said to her. 'It's all right. He thought you were someone else, that's all.'

'That's all!' the woman shrieked.

'This man attacked me!'

'Of course he didn't,' Emma protested.

'Look at my arm then.' Red finger-marks showed bright against her pale skin.

'I'm sorry. I really am,' Alex was murmuring.

'It was all a mistake,' Emma insisted to the woman. 'You look so much like my husband's first wife, you see . . . '

The crowd surrounding them was growing, heads pressing forward to see what was happening, rumours spreading.

'That man brutally attacked that poor soul.'

'Right in broad daylight too.'

'Never safe anywhere nowadays.'

Emma was tugging Alex towards the car.

'What about my arm?' the woman said aggressively, thrusting it forward again.

'You'll be all right,' Emma declared, finding the keys in Alex's pocket and sliding them into the lock. As the door yawned wide, forcing people backwards, Emma pushed him inside, slamming it shut quickly.

'Don't you let him get away with it like that,' someone urged the blonde woman. 'Vicious brute.'

'I told you,' Emma said firmly, looking straight into the huddle of doubtful faces. 'It was all a mistake. Now, kindly let me get into my car.'

At the tone of her voice, people fell away slightly and Emma slipped inside, starting the engine, then with a spurt of gravel put her foot down, seeing alarmed bodies scatter as she headed for the exit. Alex sat as if carved from granite beside her, his face strained and set.

'You see, it was all in your imagination after all,' she declared, feeling a sudden surge of relief spread through her tensed body.

'That one was maybe,' he admitted woodenly.

'Oh, Alex!' Despair filled her voice.

Even now, after such a horrific incident, he still wasn't convinced. With defeat in her eyes, she pulled the car onto the side of the road. 'Please will you drive,' she requested.

'She didn't even look like Louise,' Alex was murmuring distractedly.

Emma watched his bleak face as she listened to him.

'She was taller, fatter, older . . . '

'You see now what I mean, Alex? It really is all your imagination. You're becoming obsessed with the idea that Louise is still alive.'

'Then I'll have to prove it once and for all to myself, won't I?' he announced in a desperate tone. 'And to you, Emma.'

The car shot forward into the line of traffic, raising angry horn-blowing but Alex didn't appear to notice. His foot pressed down hard on the accelerator and Emma saw the speedometer shoot alarmingly round the dial.

'Slow down, Alex,' she warned. 'You'll get us both killed.'

'Maybe that would solve all our problems,' he gritted, but she noticed he eased the speed down a little.

'I wonder how Jamie's been getting on,' she remarked, hoping to divert his thoughts.

'I wonder,' he said drily, his gaze challenging hers as if guessing her ploy, and for the rest of the journey sat in tense, brooding silence. Emma wondered just what he was thinking. It had to be of Louise, she felt certain. Louise seemed to fill his thoughts constantly now.

Jamie was sitting, cuddled up on his grandma's lap, watching television when they finally reached the bungalow. Smudges of chocolate had left tell-tale traces round his smiling mouth as he lifted his face to be kissed.

'I'll put the kettle on,' said Mrs Crawley, moving to get up and frowning slightly as she saw their strained faces.

'No need, we must get home.' Alex's tone was abrupt.

'It's getting rather late,' Emma explained. 'Alex is worried about Jamie's bedtime.'

'Once in a while won't hurt him, surely?' Mrs Crawley's blue eyes were pleading.

Emma hesitated, then caught Alex's impatient glare. 'We'd better go,' she said and saw the sympathy that flared into the older woman's expression as she smiled back at her, patting her hand.

'Well, you have to live with him, my dear, so I won't antagonise him any further. I know my son's moods only too well, I'm afraid. Heaven knows where he gets that temper from — probably because he was born in a thunderstorm, I imagine.'

'Was he?'

Mrs Crawley smiled. 'Well, that's my excuse for him anyway.'

'You won't forget my sweets, will you, grandma?' Jamie clamoured anxiously.

'It looks to me as if you've had enough sweets already, young man,'

Emma laughed, wiping his face with a tissue.

'That wasn't sweets, Emma,' he told her. 'That was chocolate cake for tea. It was all squishy and melty.'

'And you had such a big slice, you couldn't get it all into your mouth?' suggested Emma.

'I nearly did,' he replied.

On the journey home he snuggled up to Emma and murmured sleepily, 'It was a lovely day and we had sausages and orange soup and grandma made chips and then we had ice-cream with strawberries out of their garden that I helped grandpa pick.'

'Orange soup?' queried Emma.

'Mmm,' he smiled. 'Like baked beans. We had those too.'

'Oh, tomato soup,' Emma laughed. 'Is that what you mean?'

'I 'spect so,' he said, leaning closer to her. 'I do like you, Emma. You're all cuddly like grandma. I am glad daddy married you.'

Emma's arm tightened more closely

round him and she expected Alex to make some comment as well, but his back was stiff and straight and his blue eyes refused to meet hers as she stared at his reflection in the driving mirror.

Rachel's face was a mask of ice when Emma carried the sleeping Jamie into the cottage.

'You do realise the time?' she snapped.

'Yes,' Emma replied levelly. 'But his grandparents don't see a great deal of him, unfortunately, so we didn't want to rush him away too soon.'

'Huh!' Rachel snorted. 'The least the boy sees of them, the better. All they do is spoil him.'

'And why shouldn't they?' Emma retorted. 'He is their only grandchild — so far.'

Instantly she was aware of a suspicious wariness in Rachel's eyes, seeing them flicker over her slim body, knowing exactly what that look meant.

Jamie stirred in her arms and Rachel

reached out to take him, but Emma swung away, heading for the stairs.

'It's all right, Rachel. I'll put him to bed.'

Having undressed and tucked Jamie under the covers without waking him, Emma went back into the corridor, pausing as she heard noises coming from the small spare room where Alex used to sleep, and opened the door to find Rachel making up the narrow bed.

'What are you doing?'

The woman's stony eyes smiled triumphantly back at her. 'Alex said he'll be sleeping in here in future.'

The words hit Emma forcibly and she turned to run down the stairs, bursting into the lounge where Alex sat reading the newspaper.

'Why have you asked Rachel to make up that bed?'

His eyes met her shocked ones without flinching. 'It's better I sleep in there.'

'But why?' she cried, throwing herself

onto his lap, waiting for his arms to close round her and his mouth to take hers, but he sat, motionless in the chair, drawing slightly away. 'Don't you want to sleep with me any more?'

Her fingers caught at his neck, raising his chin, compelling his eyes to meet hers and give her the answer.

'No, Emma,' he said abruptly, pulling her hands away and lifting her from his lap, to stand in front of him. 'No, Emma, I don't.'

She could only stay there, staring disbelievingly at his face, tears burning into her eyes and then a movement came from the doorway and Rachel's flat voice interrupted them.

'Your room is quite ready for you now, Alex.'

'You can't do this,' Emma blurted out, clutching at him, only to find her hands thrust back by his own and held firmly to her sides.

'I have to, Emma, it's the only way.'

A man of conscience, Brian had said. An honourable man, with old-fashioned and outdated morals. Was that the reason — thinking that, after all, his first wife might still be alive?

Emma lay, lost in the vast depths of the wide bed, awake and restless for most of the night, haunted by doubt, listening, waiting, hoping for Alex to come to her, but the long hours, chimed away by the grandfather clock in the echoing darkness, dragged on until the first flame-coloured strands of daylight lit the growing dawn outside her window and she finally fell asleep.

The house was silent when she woke, not one movement breaking the hollow quietness. Her head ached from the tears she'd wept and her face in the mirror was blotched and pale, her hair tangled and stiff round her cheeks.

Pulling a filmy robe round her cold body, she ran along the landing, opening the door of Alex's room, bursting in, wanting to feel the welcome clasp of his arms and know everything was all right again, but the bed was empty, its duvet neatly folded back and the pillows smooth.

With one regretful finger she stroked the white cotton, seeking the warmth of where he'd rested his head, but the material was stiff and chill like the atmosphere that hung around her. A small silver carriage clock ticked busily on the dark wood of the dressing table where the oval mirror reflected back her pallor.

Nearly ten o'clock! No wonder there was no one in the house. Why hadn't anyone woken her?

Alex would be at work by now; Rachel shopping, after taking Jamie to school. And Brian Pendower would be wondering why she wasn't at the reception desk of 'The Smugglers'.

With impatient fingers Emma tugged a comb through her hair and then turned on the shower, savouring the warmth that hung steamily round her as she soaped her body into wakefulness. She'd have some coffee when she reached the inn. There wasn't time now.

A loud knocking at the front door disturbed her as she dried herself and tucking the thick fluffy towel round her, she hurried down the stairs, leaving a damp trail of footprints.

Opening it just a crack, she found Brian standing amongst the roses clustering round the porch, a smile broadening his face as he stared back at her.

'Emma! You had me worried. You're always so punctual. Are you ill or something?'

She widened the door, inviting him in, hating the way his eyes travelled over her, taking in the hastily clutched towel and beads of water still gleaming on her shoulders.

'I . . . I overslept, that's all,' she stammered, pulling the towel more closely round her.

'Delectable,' he breathed. 'Alex is a very lucky guy. I only hope he realises it.'

Emma's mouth tightened, remembering the separate rooms. 'I won't be a minute, if you'd like to sit down, Brian. I'll just go up and finish dressing.'

'Need any help?' There was a hint of teasing in the suggestion which she didn't bother to answer as she hurried from the room.

★ ★ ★

'I haven't seen the new furniture you were telling me about.' Brian's voice from behind her in the bedroom made her jump as she struggled to do up the long zip fastening the back of her cotton dress. 'Here, let me do that for you.'

Before she could draw away, one hand was on her shoulder, the other resting at the base of her spine against the bareness of her skin.

'It's all right, I can manage,' she said, twisting away from him and tugging the zipper quickly into place.

His gaze flickered round the room,

lingering on the wide bed as if noticing the smoothness of one undented pillow.

'So this is the new bed,' he commented, going across and sliding his fingers along the length of the mattress. 'Is it comfortable?'

She nodded, picking up one thin-strapped sandal and pulling it onto her bare foot. 'Fine, thanks.'

'It looks remarkably unruffled after the night of unbridled passion I'm sure you and Alex must have had.'

Emma felt the colour rush to her cheeks and was trying to find a suitable answer when she heard the kitchen door open and footsteps begin to climb the stairs.

Rachel — returned from the village shops.

A wave of panic surged over her. The bedroom door wasn't closed and she heard the footsteps pause outside, then saw Rachel's spiteful eyes reflected in the mirror of her dressing-table, before they moved away again and the footsteps continued into her own room.

'What a disappointment,' Brian grinned wickedly, clearly reading her expression, 'being disturbed when life held such promise too.'

As they walked down the narrow flower-bordered front path into the lane, Emma glanced upwards and saw Rachel's face watching them through the diamond-paned window, a slight curve of malice tilting her thin lips.

'I'll make up the extra time in my lunch hour,' Emma said, turning to Brian as they went towards the harbour.

'No need at all, my dear,' he replied easily. 'Besides, I enjoy eating with you. It's the one highlight of my day.'

From the start it had become a routine that Emma ate her lunch with Brian, sitting outside on the patio if it was sunny or at one of the little tables near the bar. Really she would have been quite happy with a sandwich at her desk, but Brian insisted she should stop and eat properly, producing little delicacies not always on the menu that they shared together.

'Then I shall phone Rachel and ask her to collect Jamie, so that I can stay on later this afternoon.'

'Don't be so ridiculous! Good gracious, my dear, am I such a slave-driver? I can assure you I get far more pleasure from having you here than is justified by the meagre wage I pay; and today, that pleasure has already been enhanced a thousand-fold.'

Emma knew from the look on his face that he was referring to when she'd appeared at the door straight from the shower and didn't know how to counter his remark, but he laughed and smoothed her wrist lightly.

'Don't be so embarrassed. It's not the first time I've seen a lady clad only in a towel or even less — although I must admit the sight of you was far more delectable than most. What made you oversleep though? I could under-stand it if Alex had still been there, but he roared past me in his car soon after seven this morning when I was coming back from my swim. Racing off to work so early isn't exactly my idea of marital bliss.'

'We had a disagreement,' Emma admitted. 'After going to Cotehele yesterday. Alex thought he saw Louise again.'

'Louise!' Brian stopped and stared at her in surprise.

'I know,' Emma said wearily. 'It's not the first time this has happened. Whenever Alex sees a blonde dressed in blue, he gets the same impression, that it must be Louise. It's growing worse too. He's getting almost fanatical. I thought he was going to be arrested yesterday, grabbing at some poor woman.'

'And this keeps happening?' Brian mused thoughtfully.

'Three or four times now, when I've been with him. And not only that, on one occasion Jamie thought it was his mother too.'

'Jamie?'

Emma nodded.

'But he was only a little chap, scarcely more than a baby, when Louise was drowned.'

'I know, but somehow the memory of her has stuck in his mind. As soon as he saw the blonde hair and blue dress, he was half-way out of the burger bar, going frantic.'

'Well, I know from experience that Louise was quite something. Once you'd seen her, it was impossible to forget her ever again. But she's been dead for nearly three years now.'

'Try telling that to Alex. I'm beginning to wonder if he should see a doctor or someone. He seems to have such a terrible guilt complex.' Emma looked desperately into Brian's eyes. 'He thinks he murdered her, you know.'

'Murdered her!'

'You know what happened, don't you, Brian? Alex told me you were there. Please tell me your version,' she implored.

'What did Alex say?'

'That he found you and Louise in

one of the caves,' Emma said reluctantly. 'And Jamie waiting near the cliff-edge.'

They'd reached the inn now but Brian caught her arm and steered her down onto the beach, walking her slowly over the thin grey stones of the shingle towards the sand.

'We'd been having an affair for quite a while,' Brian admitted. 'I told you before that Louise was the kind of woman no one man could ever satisfy and Alex . . . well, from what I gather he's not exactly the great lover, is he?'

Emma wasn't sure she could agree with that, but as Alex was the only man she'd ever made love to, decided maybe she wasn't in a position to say so.

'Louise was insatiable.' Brian's face had a strange, almost wistful, look as he remembered. 'I knew I was only one of many, but it didn't matter. I didn't care. She was the most fantastic woman I've ever met.'

He gave Emma a sidelong glance and

smiled silkily, 'And I can assure you I've met quite a few in my time, my dear . . . Our affair started almost accidentally — or so it seemed at the time. I was walking along the beach, as I always do each morning, when Louise suddenly emerged from the sea.'

Emma felt his grip on her arm tighten.

'She was totally naked — how she always swam — like a beautiful mermaid, sleek and voluptous. She had a marvellous body. Perfect in every detail — and she knew it, and used it.' His lips stretched into a thin line. 'There was no way I could resist such open invitation — not that I wanted to — but Alex was my friend and I do have some morals. After that, we met early every morning but eventually, even that wasn't enough for Louise, so later she would take Jamie for a walk, leaving him on the cliff-top, and meet me again. Those caves are very secluded,' he declared.

'But didn't you worry about Jamie?'

Brian stared at her blankly. 'Why should I? He wasn't my concern.'

'Not your concern!' Emma protested, standing still and turning to face him. 'A tiny child like that, alone on the cliffs! What sort of man are you? He could have wandered off, fallen, anything.'

'Louise wasn't bothered. She assured me he always did as he was told and I'd seen him there myself, sitting on the grass, quite contented to wait for his mother to return.'

Was every male who came in contact with Louise under her spell? Emma wondered. Even little Jamie?

'And what happened — the day Louise was drowned?'

'We met as usual. Louise looked even more beautiful, if that was possible. So ripe. Utterly desirable. I couldn't wait to make love to her. And then Alex stormed onto the beach, blazing at her, dragging that poor bewildered child with him. He has a foul temper, my dear.'

'Not surprising, in the circumstances,' Emma retorted.

'When I appeared, he tore into me, both with his tongue and his fists. Well, brawling on the beach isn't something I enjoy, so I left them to it and came on back. I have a reputation to maintain in the village.'

'Which brawling would ruin, but adultery would not?' Emma enquired acidly.

'As they were both connected at the time, neither would have done my reputation any good,' Brian replied stiffly.

'And then?' urged Emma.

'Well, the next I knew was later on that day when I heard a search had been set up to look for Louise. To be honest, I thought it was all rather a waste of time. After all, a woman like that wasn't going to hang around after being treated in such a manner by her husband, when there were a thousand or more men only waiting to make it up to her, was she?'

'And Alex? Did you see him?'

Brian gave a short laugh. 'You must be joking! See Alex? After he'd given me a bloody nose? I wasn't sure he hadn't broken it.'

'And Louise's body was found eventually.'

'Quite a while after. She was trawled up in one of the fishing nets. Not a pretty sight I gather either.'

'Alex had to identify her.'

'That's right. Poor chap. I didn't much envy him then, I can tell you. After days in the sea, too. The fishes aren't fussy, you know.'

'But there was an inquest?' she said.

'Yes, and Louise was identified from what remained of her clothing. Her face, you see . . . '

Emma gave a shudder.

'I was one of the witnesses to what she was wearing that morning — not that it was a great deal.'

'But I thought you said she always swam naked?' Emma questioned.

'She did, but afterwards . . . well, she

had to collect Jamie and get back to the house, didn't she? She always slipped on a bikini. And that was what she'd been wearing when I last saw her. A tiny scrap of bright blue fabric was still clinging to her thighs when they found her apparently.'

'So everyone knew about your secret assignations with her after all?' Emma said.

'Unfortunately, yes.'

'And yet your reputation is still intact? You still run the inn.'

'There was a great deal of envy generated; and anyway, people soon forget.'

'How smug!' Emma declared contemptuously.

'It depends on how you look at it — and whether you're a male or female. As I've said, Louise was very attractive and any man who possessed her was bound to be regarded with envy. I know. I once envied Alex, until I realised exactly what it must be like, every man lusting after your wife and she only too happy to comply.'

'Was there any doubt at the inquest?'

'Whether it was Louise or not?' Brian asked. 'I don't recall any at the time. No other woman had been reported missing on this stretch of coast. She was the right age and height. And of course there was the scrap of material. Louise had perfectly flawless skin, no identifying marks like moles or scars, to my expert knowledge, so that was all there was to go on. The coroner seemed satisfied. Are you?'

He faced her squarely, looking intently into her eyes.

'We'd better be getting back to work,' Emma suggested, turning her head away to walk across the sand towards the inn where morning visitors were already gathering with their coffee on the patio.

'Perhaps we should,' Brian agreed.

'I'd hate your reputation to be sullied once again,' she added silkily.

'How thoughtful of you, my dear,' Brian observed, 'but once again, I'm sure it would only generate a great deal of envy. After all, we're all beginning to appreciate what excellent taste Alex Crawley has when it comes to choosing his women — with one exception, of course.'

Emma looked at him with suddenly curious eyes and he answered her unspoken question with a cynical smile.

'Rachel, of course. But then, they do say it's the exception that proves the rule, don't they?'

'What do you mean?' Emma asked faintly, feeling the sun hot on the back of her neck.

'Well, Alex has lived in that cottage with Rachel for several years — and for the past three all alone together. I don't think you can really count Jamie as a chaperone somehow, can you? A woman's a woman in the deep, darkness of the night, however she may appear to be in the day: and Alex is a virile young man, as I'm quite sure you're fully aware, Emma.'

With another smile, Brian bent to

kiss her cheek lightly, then opened the door and went over to the bar, greeting a couple of holiday-makers effusively, before his glittering eyes turned to her again.

'I should have a coffee, Emma. You look as if you need some.'

# 9

*Rachel*. The name whirled round and round in Emma's brain, branding itself into it. *Rachel and Alex*. It wasn't possible. But maybe Brian was right. A woman was a woman — and Alex had been on his own for a long time.

The idea worried at her for the rest of the morning, heightened every time she saw Brian watching her from his place behind the bar.

Was that why Rachel hated her so much? Because she'd taken her place in Alex's affections? And was that why Alex wouldn't get rid of her?

After all, Rachel wasn't old. Hardly older than Alex. Just because she dressed plainly and made herself look so drab . . .

But Alex wouldn't have married her and brought her to live there, knowing such a thing — or would he? Did a man care about such niceties?

Alex wasn't like that. She knew him too well. But she didn't really know him at all, did she? Only that she loved him — and thought he loved her too. Now even that was in doubt.

Separate rooms.

Another seed of doubt began to grow in her mind, rapidly. Was that so he could, once again, be with Rachel?

The midday sun beat in through the window onto her back, sending a trickle of dampness creeping past her breasts. Alex didn't love her. Never had loved her. Oh, he'd wanted her, that was true enough, but as for loving her, really loving her, she knew now that had all been a futile dream.

So what was the point of staying any longer? Rachel hated her. Alex no longer wanted her and was obsessed by visions of his first beautiful wife. Why not admit it had all been a terrible mistake and return home? Henry Cavendish would probably welcome her with open arms and she knew her parents would only be too pleased to have her back near them again.

A small fair child with deep blue, wistful eyes floated into her mind. Jamie. How could she leave him?

But children soon forget. She hadn't been there long enough for him to form any permanent attachment to her, had she? And yet, his life had been upturned once before: what would happen a second time?

She'd grown to love the little boy so much and he was beginning to trust and love her too. Could she just abandon him? And wouldn't that please Rachel; knowing she held the reins in her own hands once more?

'Lunch is waiting for you, Emma.'

Brian's smooth voice echoed in her ears and she looked up for a second without seeing him, before pushing back her hair from her eyes and rising to her feet. The sun was scorching down now, blazing in through the window and her shoulders burned from its heat.

'There's a breeze outside on the patio. We'll eat out there,' he suggested, taking her arm and directing her through the French windows into the dazzling light.

'I don't want any lunch, I'm not hungry,' she said, reluctant to be in his presence.

'Don't be childish, Emma. I know you didn't have any breakfast, and you left your coffee to go cold earlier, so you must have something now. I don't want you fading away in front of me, and then have to face the wrath of that husband of yours. I know what he can be like.'

Emma sank listlessly onto the white metal chair, thankful for the welcome shadow of the huge umbrella encircling the table and stared down at the curved glass dish resting in front of her. Cool slivers of cucumber and huge prawns deep in a creamy sauce were half-hidden in crisp shreds of lettuce, tempting her. She picked up her spoon and began to eat.

'That's better,' Brian smiled, filling a tall long-stemmed glass with sparkling white wine, ice clinking against the rim. 'Now, drink this down. It will relax you.'

Her still dazed eyes stared back at him almost uncomprehendingly as she obediently drank her wine and watched the frosted bottle tilt again.

Brian deftly replaced her empty glass dish with a plate of lemon sole, the fine white meat of the fish almost melting in her mouth as she ate it, then a lime sorbet that prickled on her tongue.

'Better?' he asked gently, tipping the final drops of the wine into her glass.

She nodded, her eyes heavy now, the numbing pain in them smoothing away as she tilted the wine-glass to her lips.

'How about a walk along the beach before you start work again? It's cool in the shade of the cliffs.'

Emma swayed slightly as she rose to her feet, her fingers gripping the edge of the table. That sun on the back of her neck, she remembered. Much too hot. I should have pulled down the blind a little, she thought.

Her heels wavered on the paved stone and bending, she slipped off her sandals, carrying them in one hand, feeling the stones burn the soles of her feet until she reached the welcome dampness of the sand.

Brian's arm was guiding her into the long shadows that reached below the dark granite of the cliffs and she leaned gratefully against his side. Her head felt heavy, a dull throb pulsing across her brows. Too much sun, that's what it was. And tears.

She could feel the hardness of Brian's hip-bone press against hers as they moved over the smoothness of the sand. Why couldn't Alex like Brian? He was so kind, so very kind and thoughtful, reminding her in some ways of her father. He'd always been the one to soothe her when she was unhappy, cuddling away her sadness.

Brian's fingers were stroking up over the bend of her elbow to her shoulder, smoothing their way along her neck to the very base of her skull, massaging away the tension and pain.

She leaned her head back against his palm.

They were passing the fallen path leading down to the beach now, skirting the scattered rocks that were strewn over the sand and above she could see the tall grasses waving along the edge of the cliff. That was the place Jamie refused to pass, the place where he'd always sat, waiting for Louise.

Emma peered sideways through half-closed eyes. The caves. Somewhere here were the caves.

A coolness surrounded her as she moved languidly into their darkness, the brightness of the sun hidden by moist rock.

Brian's fingers were sliding softly down her spine, making it tingle with excitement where they touched her skin. Her body stiffened, sensing the parting of her dress as the zip crept down her back, the sure, purposeful warmth of his hand moving round to cup her breast, and she writhed away, suddenly aware of what was happening.

'Let go of me!'

'Oh, Emma.' His voice was like honey, sweet and soft. 'You know you don't mean that. You can't fool me.'

Frantically she tried to push away, feeling her nipples tauten under his practised touch, his mouth meeting hers, his tongue forcing its way through her tightening lips, his teeth biting down.

With a swift convulsive movement, she brought her knee upwards, hearing the gasp of pain as he instinctively released her, his body doubling into a curve. Then he was reaching out again, his mouth curling into a half-smile in the dim light of the cave.

'So you're going to make me fight for it, are you? Well, that only makes things more exciting.'

Her bare feet slithered on wet fronds of seaweed as she jerked away, falling against the cold damp rock as she struggled to escape, the breath sobbing in her throat.

And then she was in daylight, the full heat of the sun blazing round her like a gigantic flame, running, running . . .

Alex's arms caught her, held her, his searing blue eyes glaring into hers as he stood, staring down to where her dress hung away from her body, almost to her waist.

'Oh, Alex. Thank goodness,' she cried, only to feel him thrust her sideways, his gaze flickering over her with pure hatred.

'Did I disturb your beach games, Emma?' His voice stung her like a whiplash. 'Rachel told me how she'd found you and Brian in our bedroom this morning . . . '

Emma couldn't believe the bitterness in his tone.

'And to think I've spent hours hating myself for my behaviour yesterday and came back to ask you to forgive me. You to forgive me! What a joke! And is your lover skulking in there, scared out of his wits like last time?'

'Alex,' Emma pleaded. 'You've got everything wrong. I was trying to get away from Brian.'

His gaze raked over her, his fingers catching at her dress, tearing the fine cotton material completely from her shoulders.

'Perhaps you didn't realise he prefers his women naked, Emma. Now, maybe you won't have to try so hard.'

With one last glowering look, Alex strode away across the sand, climbing the steps two at a time, not even pausing to glance back at her; and Emma stood, tears sliding relentlessly down her cheeks, the torn remnants of her dress clutched across her breasts, watching him go.

'I'm sorry.' Brian was standing beside her.

'You're sorry!' Her voice was barely a whisper. 'Twice you've wrecked Alex's life — and now mine as well. How can you just be sorry?'

'Emma — ' His hand caught at her

arm, but she shook it free, giving him a look of such fury that he stepped back, staring at her in horror. 'What are you going to do, Emma?'

'Do?' she demanded. 'Oh, don't worry, I shan't drown myself in the sea like Louise. Nothing so simple, I'm afraid. No, Brian, thanks to you my marriage is completely over. If it makes any difference to you, I'm going to gather up my things and return to London by the earliest possible train.'

'Don't leave like that, Emma. Alex will come round in time — once he sees reason. Look, why don't you come back to 'The Smugglers' with me and stay there. We've a couple of rooms empty. You can have one of those.'

'And be nice and near for whatever else you have in store for me? No, thank you, Brian. I'm leaving Cornwall: and the sooner I do that, the better it will be for all of us.'

'And Jamie?' Brian's voice was soft.

'You certainly know how to kick low, don't you?' Emma retorted bitterly.

'Jamie managed quite well before I came. I'm sure he'll do so again.'

But her words were bravado and the thought of the child's reaction to her going burned into her like a smouldering brand.

If she was quick, she could be gone before Jamie came home from school. With flying bare feet, Emma ran to the steep wooden steps and began to climb.

In all the excitement she hadn't realised quite how late it was and she was half-way through her packing when she heard Jamie's high voice when he ran in through the front door.

'But why didn't Emma come to meet me? I didn't want you, Rachel. I wanted her to. She always meets me. I've made her a picture.'

His footsteps were coming up the stairs now and Emma swiftly pushed the case onto the floor as the child burst into the room, flinging his arms round her knees and hugging her.

'Why didn't you come, Emma?

Rachel said you were going away. You're not, are you? I don't want you to go anywhere. I love you, Emma. More than anything else in the whole world. Even grandma and grandpa. You won't go, will you?'

'I have to, Jamie,' she replied quietly, sitting on the bed and pulling the little boy onto her lap.

'But I don't want you to,' he protested, his arms reaching up to pull her face round to his, his fingers touching the tears that scalded her cheeks. 'Don't you love us any more?'

'Of course I love you, Jamie. I'll always love you,' she choked, burying her head in his fair hair, unable to meet the heartbreak in those eyes so like his father's.

'Then why must you go?'

There was a creak of floorboards on the landing outside her door and Emma wondered whether it was Rachel, or Alex, listening there. Whoever it was, no one entered the room.

'Mummy went away and never came

back again. I don't want you to do that, Emma.'

How could she explain? Make him understand that whatever happened, she'd still love him, that she wasn't going away in the manner Louise had done?

And yet really, to a child, it was exactly the same. There was no way Emma could come back. She would be going out of his life for ever — just like Louise. A child so young could never understand the difference between death and desertion.

Jamie was clinging to her now with desperate fingers, tangling them into her hair, her dress, his tear-wet face pressed into her cheek, sobs shaking through his small body — and Emma didn't know what to do to comfort him.

The picture he'd been holding fell, crumpled, onto the bed-covers and Emma saw it was a drawing of a family of three, mother, father and little boy. The sight of it tore into her.

If she went to Alex, pleaded with

him, tried to make him understand what had really happened . . . but what was the use? He'd seen her coming from that cave — maybe even the same cave where he'd once found Louise and Brian entwined together. What else could he think? Alex wasn't a reasonable man. He was jealous. He had a ferocious temper. Both of which had been enflamed by the sight of her, almost naked, with Brian following, his face still flushed with desire. No way would she ever convince him of anything different.

Jamie was quieter now, his body shaking with silent sobs, his tears soaking into her neck, his fingers still gripping, but his eyes were closing, worn out with all the frenzy.

Emma looked down at him. She couldn't leave now. Not today. Tomorrow she'd find some way to explain things carefully — ask Mrs Trelissick maybe. She would tell her what to do.

Gently she gathered the child into her arms and carried him down the stairs, settling him in one of the armchairs while she went into the kitchen to prepare a cool drink and some salad for his tea. Rachel was standing by the sink, the expression on her gaunt face filled with such malice and hatred that Emma felt a physical shock when she saw it.

'Jamie will soon forget you.'

'I dare say he will,' she replied evenly, 'but at the moment he's too distressed for me to go.'

'I can cope with him.'

'I've no doubt you can,' she flared, 'only maybe not in the most gentle way. Jamie needs love, Rachel. When have you ever given him that? I've never seen you once cuddle or kiss him.'

Rachel's eyes were splinters of grey — flint as she glared back at her. 'The child needs no such wasted affection. He's a boy. He has to grow up into a man.'

'And can't men show love?'

A dull flush crept up Rachel's thin cheeks and she sucked in her thin lips, forcing them into a straight line.

'I doubt you've ever known what true love is, Rachel,' Emma continued, watching the woman's face, knowing that every word she spoke was cruel, but not caring any more. 'Have you ever had a lover?'

This woman could never have slept with Alex, Emma felt sure. She was like a drained pool, only the barren rock remaining. Or was that why? Had, once, Rachel devoted all the love she possessed towards him and now . . .

Where was Alex? Emma suddenly realised she hadn't seen or heard him since she returned to the house nearly an hour before. He'd rushed away from the beach in front of her, but where had he gone? She went to the window, searching for his car outside, but the lane was empty. Maybe he'd gone back to work again.

'Alex doesn't love you,' Rachel said scornfully, as if reading her thoughts. 'He never has. Alex loves only one woman — and that woman is Louise.

You can never take her place.'

And this time Emma had no choice but to believe her. Tomorrow she would leave.

But for now there was Jamie. What was she going to do about him? There were his grandparents, of course, but it was too much to expect them to have the child for always and she knew Alex would never agree. For a short time though, just while he got used to the idea of her leaving maybe? In the morning she'd contact them — when Rachel was out of the house and couldn't overhear her plans.

'Emma!' The frantic shriek brought her running into the lounge where Jamie was standing in the middle of the room, his eyes bewildered from sleep. When he saw her, he rushed into her arms, clinging desperately. 'I thought you'd gone,' he whimpered.

'No, Jamie, of course I haven't,' she answered, stroking his soft hair. Not yet.

She'd take him to school in the

morning, speak to Mrs. Trelissick and then catch the train. There was no use prolonging the agony — for both of them.

And Alex? What about him?

★ ★ ★

When he didn't return to the cottage that evening, Emma ate her meal, then climbed the stairs to finish her packing. Below the cliff she could hear the sea gently creeping over the sand, each wave clear in the still night air, dragging at the shingle. Everything was so peaceful. Through her open window the scent of roses drifted in, faint and delicate.

Why did all this have to happen? Why did Alex have to stride into her life, sweeping her away in a tumult of emotions? Why couldn't he have stayed here in Cornwall and let her remain safe in her own comfortable seclusion? Now nothing would ever be the same again. How could it? Now she knew what love was.

She heard Rachel's steps on the stairs, passing, the creak of her bedroom door before it closed. Rachel. How could a woman be so devoid of any emotion? Never once had she seen her thin face soften, never heard a tender word. Surely there must be something, or someone, who could penetrate those austere depths?

For hours she lay awake, listening for Alex's return, tensing at every car that came along the lane, waiting for one to stop and hear the welcome sound of his key in the door, his footsteps in the hall.

Then she'd go to him, make him understand. And he would understand. He had to. She didn't want to leave him. She loved him too much.

But if he did return, she didn't hear him, waking from deep troubled dreams to find yet another cloudless sky and the air already heavy with a humid, sultry heat.

Jamie was quiet at breakfast, leaning against her as he did when anxious, his eyes constantly gazing up into hers. When she took his hand to walk him to school, he clung to her fingers like a limpet and at the gates she had great difficulty persuading him to go inside with the other children.

'You won't be gone, will you, Emma?'

What could she say?

With trembling lips she bent to kiss him, hating the lie. 'No, Jamie, I won't be gone,' and watched his face break into a smile as he ran to join the others clustered round Mrs Trelissick.

How am I going to talk to her? Emma pondered. I must though. I need her help. Only she can cope with Jamie.

'Mrs Trelissick!' she called, but at that moment the bell rang and the shrieking mass of children swarming in the playground suddenly became six straight lines, marching in through the door, and the teacher was gone.

Emma walked slowly back up the hill. She hadn't told Brian she was leaving, but surely he must realise, after what had happened, that she couldn't go back to 'The Smugglers'. Her eyes skimmed the little car park at the back. Had Alex spent the night there? She was sure he hadn't returned to the cottage.

The sun burned down. Even the surface of the lane was hot, striking up through the thin soles of her sandals. Her body was drenched in sweat. The train didn't leave until later in the morning. Maybe if she had a swim . . .

When she opened the front door, the coolness of the hall was welcome. Yes, a swim before she went would make her feel better. Swiftly she ran up the stairs to slip into her bikini.

On the landing she paused. Rachel's door was not quite closed. Was she in there, lurking like a spider in its web? Emma listened, hearing only her own breathing. Gently she pushed against the wood.

A blaze of colour met her, dazzling bright in the sunshine that flooded the whole room. Every wall was painted scarlet. The ceiling too. Even the duvet on the bed and the pillows were the same brilliant shade of red. She couldn't believe it. Rachel was so drab, always wearing browns, or greys.

Once she was used to the garish glare, she realised that photographs glazed in bright red frames filled every bare surface of the room, window-sills, dressing-table, chest of drawers. Rows and rows of pictures, exactly the same, all of one woman. Louise.

From every corner, every angle of the room, Louise smiled at her. Louise with her golden-hair heavy round her shoulders, dressed in blue, a deep peacock colour. The whole room was a shrine to her. But why the same picture?

And on a hanger, tucked behind the door, was a dress in that shade of blue.

Emma stared at it, recognising it. The wide slashed neck, the full skirt, the elbow-length sleeves. It was the dress the woman in the photographs was wearing: the dress the woman on the cliff had worn: the dress the woman in Falmouth had worn: the dress the woman on the pleasure boat had worn. The same dress.

On the top of the chest of drawers was a cardboard box. She stood looking down at it, then in one swift movement lifted the lid, her fingers trembling as they reached inside, touching the softness of the smooth sleek blonde wig lying there.

*Rachel.*

Gaunt, forbidding Rachel had dressed herself in these things. But why? Was she obsessed by Louise too? Or was there another reason? Could she hate Alex so much?

Emma slipped the lid carefully back on the box. From the window she could see Rachel climbing the hill from the village, a basket over one arm. Any second she'd turn in through the gate and be here.

With one more horrified glance round at the gallery of photos, Emma closed the door and ran back along the landing to her own room, rummaging through her case to find her bikini and slipping into it.

She could hear Rachel in the kitchen and knew there was no way of avoiding her when she went through and out into the garden to get to the beach.

Rachel's eyes flickered over her, the thin lines of her mouth tightening.

'Will you meet Jamie from school this afternoon, Rachel? I shall be gone by then.'

Was there a faint glimmer of pleasure in those flint-like grey eyes? Emma wondered.

'You're swimming, now?' Rachel's flat voice sounded surprised.

'I thought it would cool me down before the train journey. It won't take long to dry my costume in this heat. And I wanted, one last time, to remember . . . ' Emma's voice died away.

To remember the happiness. The happiness that once she shared with Alex, together there on the sand, swimming, lazing in the sunshine, thinking then that he'd loved her.

With a determined lift of her chin, she gulped back her tears and went out into the garden, shivering at the morning dew where the lawn was still shaded by the thick walls of the cottage, as it brushed her bare toes, chilling them for a second or two until she reached the field on the cliff-top.

She could see the sand below her, shimmering with haze, the sea creaming lazily over the shoreline where a dark line of seaweed drifted to and fro. Her feet burned now from the heat of the path as she came to the place where it had fallen away, and scrambled down. Pink cushions of thrift clustered the cliff-edge and bees droned as they nuzzled their way into the sweet softness.

Somewhere a grasshopper clicked in the long grass.

Everything was so perfect. How can I ever leave all this? Emma thought, her heart almost breaking with sadness. I love everything about the place — and I love Alex.

The grey flat stones of the shingle crunched beneath her weight, shifting slightly as she moved over them to meet the scorching heat of the sand that changed to cool dampness before tiny waves reached out to catch at her.

She wandered through the shallow water, strands of seaweed trailing round her ankles, tiny shells pricking her toes. She didn't want to go away.

Nearer the rocks the sea was stronger, sending pillars of spray high into the air as it pounded against them. She felt a fine mist settle on her heated skin, salty to the questing tongue she ran over her dry lips.

It was cool here in the shelter of the cliffs and she perched herself on one smooth rock, her feet deep in the swirling water, feeling it reach to her knees as the waves heaved their ponderous way towards her.

She closed her eyes, trying to blot out her unhappiness.

Alex.

Her whole being ached for him.

An icy hand gripping her ankle startled her, making her almost slip from the surface of the rock.

Rachel's sea-wet face was staring back at her.

# 10

She sat quite still, the chill of Rachel's fingers freezing her skin, watching slow rivulets of water meander down the woman's wrist. The sun seemed suddenly cold, cold as the menace in the stone-grey eyes piercing their way into hers.

'What do you want?' It was a silly thing to say, but Emma's brain was paralysed, fear inching its way through her.

'You've been prying.'

'What do you mean?'

Rachel's mouth widened into a smile that only enhanced the sharpness of her face. 'Don't play games, Mrs Crawley. You were in my room, weren't you?' The fingers dug more deeply. 'No one goes into my room.'

'The door was open,' Emma stammered. 'I went to close it and . . . '

'And couldn't resist the temptation to go inside. So, what did you find, Mrs Crawley?'

'The colour did surprise me,' Emma said.

'Colour?'

'Your walls. The bed covers. That scarlet. It was something I didn't expect of you.'

'Oh, there's a great deal you don't know about me, Mrs Crawley.'

Each time she said the name, she emphasised it, her nails digging into Emma's chilled skin, drawing the words out as if enjoying the sound of them.

'Somehow I doubt that, Rachel,' Emma remarked quietly.

The woman's eyes narrowed and with one swift movement, she hauled herself onto the rock beside Emma, her thin body in its black bathing costume as gaunt and angular as her face.

'You try to hide your real self, don't you, Rachel? Pretending to be someone else. But who are you? The drab plain woman we see every day, or the flamboyant blonde in the peacock-blue dress?'

Rachel's eyes burned into hers, her sallow skin flushing angrily. 'So you did pry into my things. How dare you!'

'I couldn't avoid seeing all those photographs, could I? No wonder Jamie has never forgotten his mother. Did you make him look at them too? Keep her memory alive for him, as you did for yourself. And as for that dress: why didn't you hide it away, if you didn't want anyone to see it and know?'

All fear was gone from Emma now, only a burning anger, knowing how this woman had tortured Alex, almost destroying him — and their marriage. 'Why did you do it, Rachel? Do you hate Alex so much?'

A strange look filled the grey eyes until they almost softened. 'Hate him? Alex? I love Alex. Don't you realise that? I've always loved Alex, ever since we were children. And then Louise came along with her golden-hair and beautiful body.'

Rachel's mouth twisted horribly and Emma could only stare at her in amazement, listening to the bitter words that streamed out in one torrent of venom.

'I hated Louise. Hated what she was doing to Alex. But he still loved her. He didn't even notice me. Then, when I came to work here, I thought things would change. Being there, side by side, together — he had to know how much I loved him. And seeing us, too, he'd realise there was no comparison between Louise and me. She was a slut. Why didn't he realise?' The sentence was torn from her in a wail of misery and agony. 'But I knew that when she'd gone, Alex would change — and I'd be there. I'd be the one he'd turn to. He would love me.'

Heavy dark clouds were gathering over the clifftop now, hiding the sun and Emma hunched her body, feeling a shiver run down her spine, despite the sultry heat.

'It didn't happen though, did it?' she

242

prompted. 'Alex married me.'

The grey eyes glittered back at hers. 'You, with your red-gold curls. Another golden-haired woman — like her.'

'So you decided to dress like Louise, to follow Alex, to torment him, punish him for not loving you . . . '

'No!' The word was a cry of anguish. 'I would never hurt Alex.'

'Then why did you do it, Rachel, going wherever he went, pretending to be Louise? Surely you must have known what it would do to him?'

'Alex loved Louise. If I look like her, Alex will love me. He will, he will.'

She's mad, Emma thought, hearing the hysterical shriek rise high into the air.

'Alex will love me.' There was a finality in those words, a purpose that filled Emma with a sudden terror. 'And only me.'

'Yes, Rachel.' She was humouring her now, trying to quell the fear twisting through her own body. 'Alex will love you. Once I've gone away,

Alex will love you.'

'But you'll come back.' The thin, sinewy fingers were tight on her arm. 'You'll come back and when he sees you, all golden-haired and beautiful . . . but I won't let you do that. I wouldn't let Louise and I won't let you.'

'What do you mean? You wouldn't let Louise?'

Rachel's lips were smiling again now, her eyes filled with a sudden humour. 'Didn't you realise? I killed Louise.'

'You!'

'I told Alex where he'd find her that day. I'd seen her down there on the beach, heard her in that cave, with Brian Pendower — and others. It was the slut's favourite place. And then I went after him. I wanted to be there, when he realised what he'd married, to be there, to comfort him. Then he'd know just how much I loved him.

'I heard him raging at them, saw him hit Pendower and the coward slink away too scared to fight back. Then

Louise began to taunt him, using foul words, describing such things, I had to close my ears. She was so vile, so obscene.

'She stood there in the water, tantalising him with that body of hers, trying to lure him after her, but he didn't go. I watched him seize the child and storm his way back up the path, not even seeing me where I stood there beneath the shadow of the cliff, waiting to comfort him. He didn't even notice me at all.' Her voice died away in a choking sob.

'I hated her then, for what she'd done to him, and I followed her into the water, right out to those rocks beyond the cliff there. I caught up with her, seizing her by that beautiful golden-hair, watching her lovely face change to ugliness as I held her down, feeling that perfect body strive against mine until all the strength went out of it. And I wedged her deep between the rocks, knowing it would take time before the sea dislodged her, and by then . . . Alex would love only me.'

'And did he?' Emma challenged, needing to know.

'He would have done — given time,' Rachel answered defensively. 'But I hadn't reckoned for the guilt that held him, blaming himself for Louise's death. I wanted to tell him that it wasn't his fault, but somehow . . . I couldn't find the words. He would have known then, you see, just how much I loved him, but I was frightened too. Alex is an honest man. He would've had to tell the police and . . . I had to be here, with him, caring for him, knowing that one day . . . '

'Rachel, we must go back to the house,' Emma said gently. 'We must find Alex and tell him. It isn't fair. He's tortured by guilt, thinking he destroyed Louise. You can't let that happen, can you, Rachel?'

'He doesn't have to know.' Her mouth was obstinate.

'You can't let him go on blaming himself, Rachel.'

'One day I'll tell him — when we're married.' Her expression changed suddenly, suspicion flooding over it. 'But you'll tell him, won't you? To win him back. You, who are just as much a slut as Louise. I saw you in your bedroom with that man Pendower yesterday morning. It's you who are the torturer, knowing how much Alex hates him. And yet you spend all your time with that lecher, even letting him into your bed.'

'Of course I didn't, Rachel. Brian called because he was worried that I hadn't turned up and thought I might be ill. He followed me to my room because he wanted to see the new furniture. Nothing happened.'

'Liar! Slut! You took him to the beach, like she used to do, to the same cave even, betraying Alex as she did.'

'It's not true, Rachel.'

'You shall die as she did — slowly, so that I can enjoy watching you.'

With a sudden lunge, Rachel pushed her forward and Emma felt the surge of the sea catch her body, tugging at her, then strong fingers caught at the slender column of her neck, dragging her down.

A rush of salt water filled her mouth, choking her, tearing away every scrap of breath, scalding her eyes. Her arms fought against the grip closing round her, her feet kicking out in terror, her elbow meeting the taut hardness of Rachel's stomach, feeling it jerk away.

With a gasp of relief, her face broke the surface, sucking in the warm air, before the grasping fingers tore at her again, forcing her back down into a terrible pressure that roared in her ears and began to blacken her brain.

There was no way she could escape. Rachel's wiry strength was too great.

Pain seared her back, the cruel sharpness of the rocks, driving her into consciousness and she twisted away to grasp the rough surface, hauling herself frantically upwards.

Again the fresh sweet air swirled round her as she clung, gulping in great lungfuls, kicking sharply at the hands threatening to entrap her once more. Hands that caught at her, lifting her, holding her, before she fell into a deep black void.

Alex's blue gaze was burning into her, his fingers tenderly stroking her cheek when she slowly raised heavy lids to stare disbelievingly back at him from the softness of her own bed.

Every inch of her body was agony, her chest and throat smarting with rawness, while her neck felt as if it had been wrenched from her shoulders. But Alex was there, the angular planes of his face sharp and taut, his eyes filled with an anguish that twisted at his mouth.

'Rachel?' The name crept through salt-dry lips.

'She swam out to sea. They're searching for her now. Just rest, Emma darling. Don't try to talk.'

His fingers were soothing her forehead, sliding lightly over her cheek and down to her chin, calming her.

Reluctantly her eyelids hovered and closed.

When she opened them again, her head was clear, the terrible pressure gone. Alex was still there, in a chair beside the bed, watching her. The time? Was it late? Jamie?

'Jamie?'

'He's with my parents. They came over yesterday to stay and look after him. Don't worry. He's fine.'

He held a glass to her lips and she drank the water thankfully, feeling it slide painfully down her parched throat.

'You came back? Where were you, Alex?'

A shadow darkened his eyes and Emma saw a nerve quiver in his tanned cheek as his jaw tensed.

'I'm sorry, Emma.'

She lifted her mouth to his, brushing his lips gently, feeling the rasp of stubble, and heard the catch in his throat as their kiss lengthened.

'I went down to 'The Smugglers' to finish things off with Pendower. It was stupid of me. I'm not a fighter, neither is he. When I stormed in, he tried to reason with me, but I didn't want to listen. I hit him. It was a satisfying sound, the crunch of my fist into his face . . . The sight of the blood brought me to my senses. This time I did break his nose.' Emma saw his lips curve slightly.

'He gave me a brandy. We both needed that. After a couple more, I lost count. I slept the night there, flat out, blind drunk. He's a strange sort of guy.

'In the morning I felt terrible. Brian explained things, how he'd made all the running and how you'd resisted. I realised then just what I'd done . . . It was late when I came back here and found your case, packed. From the window I could see you and Rachel out on the rocks. It seemed odd to me, that disliking each other so much, you were there together. Then, as I watched, I saw her drag you down into the water.

'Getting to the beach was the longest journey in my whole life. I was convinced you'd drown and that I'd lost you for ever. I couldn't have borne that.'

Emma slipped her hand into his, stroking his palm with her thumb.

'It was Rachel — the woman in blue,' she whispered.

'I know. We've had the police here. My parents insisted. I suppose I'd have let her get away with it, but they said it wasn't right. Poor Rachel.'

'She loves you, Alex.'

His eyes widened. 'Rachel?'

'She always has done. This was her way of showing you. She thought, if she pretended to be Louise, you could only love her.' Emma paused for a moment. 'She knew just how much you still love Louise.'

'Love Louise.' Alex gave a deep sigh. 'Is that what you both thought? Once upon a time, maybe I did. Right at the beginning, before I realised what sort of woman I'd married . . . before I met you, Emma, and knew what true love was all about.'

'I didn't think I could compete,' Emma confessed.

'Compete! There was no competition. As soon as I saw you, I knew. You were the only woman I wanted, the one woman I've always wanted. Why else do you think I rushed you off your feet, not giving you a chance to even think? Not telling you . . . '

He bent forward, burying his head against hers.

'We're meant to be together. I love you, Emma,' he said. 'And when I saw you with Jamie, the way you loved him and he loved you, then I loved you even more.'

He picked up a crumpled paper from the bedside table where she'd placed it, smoothing it out carefully. 'I'm not the only one to think that either.'

Emma's eyes blurred as she looked at Jamie's drawing once again, seeing the three figures on the page. One darkly crayoned, tall and thin with matchstick legs, the second dressed in a yellow triangular skirt and the third, much,

much, smaller, standing in the middle holding both their hands, widely smiling.

In black felt-tip wobbling across the bottom of the paper were two words: MY FAMLEE.

'Will he mind when we include a pram?' Emma asked.

'Ask him yourself,' Alex smiled, moving to the window at the sound of voices in the lane.

There was a rush of noise over the polished boards of the hall, then a scampering up the stairs and finally the door burst open and Jamie stood there, flushed, his fair hair damp against his forehead, his eyes wide and anxious.

'I thought you'd gone away,' he choked, clambering onto the bed and throwing himself into Emma's waiting arms, hugging her with a force that threatened to squeeze all the breath out of her.

His gaze lifted to meet hers. 'You won't ever go, will you, Emma?'

Emma looked up at Alex to receive

her answer, and then back to the child, drawing him close, feeling the warmth of his body lean against her, the fair head brushing her chin as he tucked it into the comfort of her shoulder.

'No, Jamie, I promise I won't ever go. Not now.'

'Are we allowed to join the family party or is it exclusively for the younger members?' Mrs Crawley popped her fluffy white head round the door, her face beaming when she saw them. 'How are you feeling, my dear? You had us so worried, you know. That terrible woman . . . and to think she was in charge of our Jamie for so long.'

'Not any more, mother,' Alex said quietly.

His father joined her in the doorway, filling it with his height.

'What about this picture, young Jamie? Is that for Emma too?'

The little boy raised his eyes, shaking his head as he did so. 'No, grandpa. You can throw that in the bin.'

'Can't I look at it first?' Emma asked,

holding out her hand to take the scrap of paper, her breath catching in her throat when she saw the painting.

A small matchstick figure stood there, its head huge and white, big blue eyes almost filling the whole face, and from them dripped a steady stream of tears.

'Is that you, Jamie?' she said.

'Not any more, Emma,' he smiled. 'That was me yesterday at school — when I thought you weren't going to stay with us any more.' He snuggled his head closer to her. 'Is daddy going to come back into this bed tonight or stay in that other room on his ownsome?'

Emma felt her cheeks redden as she caught the glance that passed between Mr and Mrs Crawley, but Alex quickly sat down on the bed next to her, his arm firmly encircling them both as he said, 'Of course I shall be sleeping in here again — when Emma's quite better, that is.'

'Oh, I'm quite better,' Emma assured him, with a tremor of laughter as she gazed up into his questioning blue gaze.

'I think maybe it's time you came downstairs and had your tea, Jamie dear,' Mrs Crawley hurriedly interrupted, seeing the expression that was spreading over her son's handsome face. 'We'll leave your daddy to look after Emma for a while — and make sure she gets plenty of rest.'

'Well, now,' said Alex, as he drew Emma into his arms, 'what was it you were saying a little while ago about a pram . . . '